T0086217

THE
DEFECTOR

PREVIOUS BOOKS BY ALAN REFKIN

Fiction

Matt Moretti and Han Li Series
The Archivist
The Abductions
The Payback
The Forgotten
The Cabal
The Chase

Mauro Bruno Detective Series
The Patriarch
The Scion
The Artifact
The Mistress

Gunter Wayan Series
The Organization
The Frame
The Arrangement

Nonfiction

The Wild Wild East: Lessons for Success in Business in Contemporary Capitalist China
By Alan Refkin and Daniel Borgia, PhD

Doing the China Tango: How to Dance around Common Pitfalls in Chinese Business Relationships
By Alan Refkin and Scott Cray

Conducting Business in the Land of the Dragon: What Every Businessperson Needs To Know About China
By Alan Refkin and Scott Cray

Piercing the Great Wall of Corporate China: How to Perform Forensic Due Diligence on Chinese Companies
By Alan Refkin and David Dodge

THE
DEFECTOR

*A **GUNTER WAYAN** PRIVATE INVESTIGATOR THRILLER*

ALAN REFKIN

THE DEFECTOR
A GUNTER WAYAN PRIVATE INVESTIGATOR THRILLER

iUniverse books may be ordered through booksellers or by contacting:

iUniverse
1663 Liberty Drive
Bloomington, IN 47403
www.iuniverse.com
844-349-9409

ISBN: 978-1-6632-5078-0 (sc)
ISBN: 978-1-6632-5079-7 (e)

Library of Congress Control Number: 2023902879

Print information available on the last page.

iUniverse rev. date: 02/16/2023

To my wife, Kerry
and
Dr. Charles and Aprille Pappas

Odesa, Ukraine, midnight, November 20, 2022

As the Russian Federation's P-650 midget submarine stealthily entered Ukrainian waters outside the port city of Odesa, Colonel Aleksei Assonov wanted nothing more than to get him and the other five members of his special operations team out of this pressurized tube and onto land. He had nothing against the crew or the submarine clandestinely taking them through the port and into the Dnieper River. His uneasiness stemmed from feeling helpless within the confines of the submersible and leaving his fate in the hands of others. Although the two hundred thirty-seven mile trip from Sevastopol, Crimea, was uneventful, they were now in an area ringed with anti-ship missiles, and in waters outside published sea lanes which were saturated with mines and had sophisticated undersea detection devices. The midget was supposed to be quiet enough to be undetectable to the sea lane detection devices. However, the only way he'd know if that belief was accurate was if he lived because, given the relations between both countries, they were as good as dead if discovered, as the Ukrainians weren't going to ask for their surrender.

He would have preferred to leave the submarine outside the port and use underwater scooters to take them to their target. In his experience, the scooters were so quiet that they were impossible to detect. However, because they were there to kidnap a scientist and his wife, Fedir and Olena Kuzma, both in their late fifties, the mission planners expressed significant doubt whether the scared and apprehensive couple could survive an extended underwater ride in the dark, even with cold water wetsuits, with the water at fifty-three degrees Fahrenheit. Therefore, they needed to sail up the Dnieper River to the top secret lab operated by the National Academy of Sciences where, according to the intelligence report he received, the scientist worked every day from ten at night to the following morning because he was a workaholic and believed there would be fewer distractions during these hours. His wife was said to rarely leave their home, which was in the residential development for Academy employees next to her husband's place of work. The plan was that after they brought the couple onboard, the submarine would return to Sevastopol. From there, each would be taken to a different destination.

The submarine was cruising at four mph as it crossed the eastern part of Odesa Harbour and entered the mouth of the Dnieper River. However, because the river shallowed quickly, the captain surfaced for the rest of the journey. Although that technically meant someone could see the craft, the glow of intermittent lights from shore didn't reach the center of the river, allowing the submarine to remain in darkness as it navigated through the shallow waters. One hour later, the captain stopped the craft and summoned Assonov to the bridge.

"We're at the coordinates," the captain said.

The colonel, in combat gear like the rest of his team, with night vision goggles atop his helmet, a backpack, and an AS VAL suppressed assault rifle slung over his right shoulder, shook his head in acknowledgment. "Keep your submarine here until we return," he said. "We may need a fast escape."

"Daylight is in seven hours," the captain stated. "I can't submerge until I'm nearly at the mouth of the river. If you're late, we'll be seen."

"I know, and I don't care. Don't move this vessel," Assonov said, not waiting for a response before leading his team on deck.

It was a moonless night as the special ops team brought their rigid inflatable boat, or RIB, on deck and inflated it with high-pressure air before sliding it onto the water. Once everyone was in, the helmsman turned on the fifty-hp engine, which had a top speed of thirty-seven mph.

"We're two miles away. Set a course for zero-nine-five," the colonel said as he looked at his handheld GPS device.

The helmsman gently pushed the throttle forward, adjusting the inflatable's course as the RIB silently took off.

When the inflatable coasted to a stop at a pre-determined point along the riverbank, the team stepped out and secured the RIB to a tree. Adhering to their plan, Assonov sent two men to the scientist's house while he and the other four went to the top-secret facility. That building was three stories high, well-lit, and had a uniformed guard to the left of the entrance. Surrounding it was a large plot of grass bordered by a ten-foot-high wrought iron fence with horizontal wires spaced every six inches from the ground up. In front of the fence were large plastic hexagonal signs with a lightning bolt emblazoned on them, indicating that the fence was electrified. The gravel road onto the Academy grounds, accessed through twin entry gates, was on the right side of the property and ended in a parking lot. It also had similarly spaced horizontal wires attached to it. A plastic sign affixed to the center of each gate warned it was electrified.

Assonov lifted his night vision goggles and replaced them with a pair of smart glasses to see if a laser security system protected the property. When no laser beams were detected, he again lowered his night vision goggles.

"I see four surveillance cameras," one of his men said, pointing them out to the colonel.

"Neutralize them with the IR laser," the colonel replied, referring to the infrared device that disabled cameras by freezing the lens so that its monitor would continue to show that image on the screen, making their intrusion invisible.

Once the cameras were blinded, Assonov ordered the squad's sniper to dispatch the guard, who was smoking a cigarette. At this distance, the shot was complicated because he needed to put a round between the vertical slats and the nearly invisible horizontal hot wires in the wrought iron fence. Striking either, the colonel warned, would likely set off perimeter alarms. The sniper, the oldest squad member, was used to making difficult shots, the round striking the guard in the center of the forehead.

With the guard dead, the colonel focused on which technique he needed to employ to get past the electrified fence without being detected. The first step in that process was determining how many volts it carried. The squad member tasked to give him that answer removed a digital measuring device from his backpack, placed it near the wire, and told the colonel they were looking at a ten thousand volt system.

Depending on the voltage, there are several ways to neutralize an electrified fence or gate. Given the equipment and devices his team carried, Assonov knew he had three options to get past a system with this voltage. The first was running a copper wire from the fence or gate to a metal stake in the ground. The second was placing a heavy object against either. Both would cause a short circuit, blowing a fuse and shutting down the power long enough for them to hop over. However, since this technique was well-known to those designing and installing electrified systems, engineers usually incorporated a circuit where the loss of power would trigger an alarm. Therefore, Assonov discarded the first two options, focusing on number three.

"Let's look at the access gates," he said into his headset as he walked twenty yards to his right to one of the large concrete pillars holding one up.

He and one of his men inspected the pillar closely, concluding that because they didn't see electrical cables or wires around it, and because the concrete was not a conductive material, they could scale the pillar without getting fried. "Let's check the other side," he said. Looking through the wrought iron slats, Assonov pointed to two steel posts, a plastic dome attached to each. "Motion sensors," he stated into his mic. "Who has the container?"

One of his men quickly came forward.

"Disable those sensors," Assonov ordered, pointing to them.

The special ops soldier removed a stainless steel container with a Styrofoam lid from his backpack and, with the help of other squad members, climbed the pillar and poured the liquid nitrogen over the sensors, instantly freezing and temporarily disabling them. The rest of the team followed, joining him on the gravel road.

Once past the gates, and with the cameras neutralized, the squad ran to the front door of the building, found it unlocked, and entered unopposed. Although they didn't know the location of the scientist's office, their intel report stated that he would be the only scientist working this late, the others not arriving until between eight and nine. As they entered the lobby, the colonel received a call from one of the two operators sent to the scientist's house, saying they had Olena Kuzma in custody and would take her to the RIB.

Assonov suspected there was more than one security guard for a building and grounds of this size. They would search one floor at a time, on alert for the guards, while looking for the scientist. The colonel divided his team into three groups, and they silently began their search. His assumption of additional guards turned out to be correct. His team found the Academy's security office at the end of a hallway and two uniformed guards asleep in their chairs. Unhesitatingly, he put a bullet in their heads. Seconds later, the remainder of his team reported that the floor was clear.

"Assemble at the security office," the colonel said, giving them the location.

The control panel, which had a symbol above each button showing its function, was in front of the dead guards. After inspecting it, Assonov found the one which shut off the electrification of the fence and gates and saw the reading on the power gauge below the button fall to zero after pressing it. He then pushed the green button below the gate symbol, after which he walked back to the building entrance to verify that the gates had opened. They did.

With the first floor secure, they proceeded to the second floor, found no one, and went to the third and into its only lab, which was empty. Assonov considered that odd, not only because their intelligence report stated the scientist was a workaholic and would be here at this hour, but also because, unlike the small labs on the other floors, this one dominated two-thirds of the space and had all the lights on.

"Look inside the cabinets and above the ceiling tiles," the colonel ordered.

As his men began that search, Assonov went to an LED screen monitor on the counter and saw that the screen was divided into sixteen squares, each receiving a live interior camera feed from a remote monitoring device. The lab he was in appeared in the cube on the bottom right.

"Dermo!" he explained, angry that he hadn't considered that the interior of the building would have surveillance cameras.

The scientist had no idea what the invaders wanted, but he wasn't going to stick around to find out. Upon seeing them enter the building, he grabbed his computer and backup hard drive, which contained his life's work, and put them in a weathered satchel. He then took several pieces of electronic equipment and carefully placed them inside the foam inserts in a large black roller bag. Throwing the satchel over his left shoulder and pulling the roller bag with his right hand, he raced to the staircase, which would take him to his car in the underground parking garage.

The descent took much longer than it should have because the scientist was a pack-a-day smoker and had the lung capacity of a gerbil. When he arrived at his aging ZAZ Tavria, a Ukrainian-manufactured subcompact, he opened the trunk and put the suitcase and satchel inside. Hearing footprints behind him, he turned around and saw a six-foot-one-inch tall, thick-chested man in his late thirties dressed in black fatigues and wearing a helmet with his night vision goggles flipped up. Behind him were five others who were similarly dressed. The startled scientist's mouth dropped open.

"Going somewhere?" Assonov asked in his husky voice.

Fedir Kuzma, still gasping from being out of breath, looked apprehensively at the person who asked the question.

"Home," he replied with a stutter.

"You're relocating," Assonov said.

2

Seven weeks later – January 8, 2023

The Indonesian group consisted of fifteen tourists and a guide, chosen because she was at the bottom rung of the ladder for seniority within her company. The weeklong excursion was a blitz of Moscow and Oymyakon, the coldest permanently inhabited settlement on earth, where the current temperature was minus thirty-two degrees Fahrenheit during the day, plunging to minus fifty-three at night. The Siberian enclave of four hundred fifty hearty souls, two hundred miles south of the Arctic Circle, had no commercial lodging, restaurants, airport, or train station. Historically, residents made a meager living by breeding reindeer, hunting, and ice-fishing. However, their income took a significant uptick several years ago when Tamara Egorovna heard about the hostile environment in which they lived and, with marketing genius, began advertising the town as an adventure tourist destination, with those visiting the settlement having the bragging rights of going someplace that few on earth could see. Because there were no hotels or restaurants, food and lodging were provided by residents bringing tourists into their log cabin homes, the largest being a five-room addition to a one-bedroom residence built to accommodate tour groups. The adventurers, not expecting much in the way of either food or lodging, and there for the experience and bragging rights, paid heavily for stays which typically lasted between one and two days.

The journey to Oymyakon began by flying to Moscow, staying only long enough to freshen up and get a few hours of sleep at an airport hotel before taking the first of three flights needed to get them close to the settlement, the last flight landing in Ust Nera. From there, a bus would transport everyone to Oymyakon. On their return, tour groups usually spent up to three days in Moscow before going home.

The Aeroflot Ilyushin Il-62 aircraft transporting the tourists to Moscow was a half-century old and didn't hide its age. The group, who changed planes in Saint Petersburg, boarded the two hundred fifty passenger aircraft with trepidation after seeing paint chipped from its faded white exterior and the narrow, cracked black Naugahyde seats, which had deteriorated from extensive use. Even though the average Russian wasn't svelte, the airline decided to maximize its revenue on the lucrative route by cramming as many passengers as possible onto the aircraft. Subsequently, over time, not only had the imitation leather that covered the seats deteriorated, but the padding behind it had disintegrated so that passengers felt as if their backs and asses were resting against a steel frame—which they were, comfort not being in the Russian airline's lexicon.

Three in this group were there for reasons other than tourism. Gunter Wayan and Eka Endah were private investigators and equal partners in W&E Investigations in Bali who worked from their residence. Wayan was five feet seven inches tall, had short black hair, coffee-brown skin, a medium build, and was neither heavy nor thin. Eka was a five feet six inches tall shapely brunette with an athletic body and silken hair cascading over her tawny-brown shoulders. The third non-tourist was Suton Persik, a first lieutenant in the Criminal Detective Unit of the Bali police department. He was bald, five feet ten inches tall with soft-brown skin, and had an extended stomach that displayed twenty-five pounds of unwanted weight.

Originally, Major Langit Tamala and Captain Bakti Nabar, members of the Indonesian military, were to accompany them. However, at the last minute, it was decided that having active duty military on the tour might raise a red flag with the Russians and attract the scrutiny of Russia's FSB, short for Federalnaya Sluzhba Bezopasnosti, which was the successor to the Soviet Union's KGB and the principal agency responsible for internal and border security, counterintelligence, counterterrorism, and investigating serious crimes and violations of federal law. This broad mandate gave them power over every person, institution, and entity that affects the State, subject only to the restraints placed on them by the president of the Russian Federation, to whom the FSB was solely answerable.

Because happenstance caused these non-tourists to work together in the past, overcoming situations some would have said were insurmountable, the Indonesian government asked them to come together again for a particularly sensitive assignment. The task they were given required that they go to Oymyakon and Moscow, necessitating the government put a wad of cash in the tour company's coffers to assemble this excursion in a few days, entice twelve others to join as cover by saying that they'd won the trip in a contest none remembered entering, because none did, and informing the guide that three in her group would be on a self-guided tour and to leave them alone.

When the Ilyushin landed at Moscow's Domodedovo Airport, twenty-six miles from the center of the city, the group passed through immigration and customs and went to the Aerotel Domodedovo, which was less than a mile from the airport. After checking in, Wayan called the Indonesian embassy and complained about their tour, following the instructions given him by Defense Minister David Sondoro before he left. The operator expected his call and said the person handling such complaints would meet him in two hours. Although she didn't provide the location of the meeting, before leaving Bali, Sondoro gave Wayan the Bolshoi Theater as the place where he, Eka, and Persik would rendezvous with the embassy official.

The three non-tourists had been waiting on the theater's steps for ten minutes when Persik pointed to a circular silver pin on Wayan's coat. "I've been meaning to ask you the significance of that pin."

"Eka gave it to me. It's become so automatic that I put it on that I forgot I was wearing it."

"So, it has romantic significance?"

Eka, who'd overheard the conversation, laughed. "I bought it for him because he has a habit of leaving his cell phone behind when doing errands, and I never knew where he was. Given what's happened to us recently, I thought it was a good idea," Eka responded; she and Wayan having been recently kidnapped by North Korea before being saved by the Israelis.

"It's a tracking device?"

"A domestic tracking device that only works with our cell phone carrier and won't operate outside the country. I also have one but left it at home."

Their discussion stopped when a man who was five feet five inches in height, of average weight, and in his early fifties approached and introduced himself as Kevin Tjay, the Indonesian embassy's Deputy Chief of Mission. "I understand you have a complaint about your tour," he said.

Wayan confirmed that he'd called the embassy, drawing a nod from Tjay.

"Let's go somewhere less public. Although I took steps to ensure that I wasn't followed, my face is known to the FSB. There's a quiet coffee house less than a block away where we can talk," he said, starting in that direction.

"The Russians don't follow embassy staff?" Eka questioned.

"Not unless there's a reason. I suspect they don't have the human resources because Moscow has one hundred forty-seven embassies. The FSB keeps a van with tinted windows parked 24/7 outside our embassy, which I'm of the belief they use to photograph those who enter and leave our building, although they haven't offered to give the ambassador or me a tour of what's inside," he said with a slight chuckle. "Additionally, looking through the windows of the government building across the street from my office, I can see directional antennas and parabolic dishes aimed at the embassy."

"And if we met at the embassy, we'd be photographed, and the FSB might become curious," Persik added.

"It's best to avoid the FSB whenever possible. This country is a police state, and it's better not to bring undue attention to oneself," Tjay said as he led the way into the coffee house and selected a table in the corner, which had no one seated near it.

Once the server took their order, returned with their coffee, and left, Tjay got down to business.

"Minister Sondoro told me to update you on Fedir and Olena Kuzma."

"What can you tell us?" Wayan asked.

"Let me start at the beginning, possibly repeating what you already know. Our embassy is across the street from a Russian government building. Within that structure, the FSB has built a temporary lab for Doctor Kuzma."

"How do you know he's there and that the FSB is running the show?" Persik asked.

"I have a habit of going to lunch at the restaurant next to the embassy every day at noon, largely because it's convenient, and they have nasi goreng, curry, and other Asian specialties on their menu, which I'm sure is because we're next door. Seven weeks ago, as I was sitting at a table, a man who appeared to be in his late fifties came in. Following him were two men who—by their looks, demeanor, earpieces, and that they followed the person into and out of the restaurant without ordering, I assumed to be a security detail. The man buys a coffee to-go at the counter and, as he's walking past me on his way out, drops a note. I quickly put my foot over it so the guards wouldn't notice and waited until they left the restaurant before picking it up."

"And the note?" Wayan asked, eager to hear what was on it.

"He introduced himself as Dr. Fedir Kuzma, said that he was working in a military lab across from my embassy, and that he and his wife wanted to defect to Bali."

"Did the defector's note say anything else?" Eka asked.

"It went on to say that he knows I work at the embassy because, from his lab window, he sees me leave the embassy and go into the restaurant at noon every day. He asks that we start exchanging messages, telling me to leave mine in the insulation sleeve of his coffee cup. He said he'll order coffee at the same time every day and will continue to drop notes."

"How could you hide a message in the insulation sleeve? Aren't they usually stacked on the counter with whoever is working that day putting the sleeve on the cup?" Eka asked.

"The restaurant staff knows me because I eat there every day. It wasn't difficult to bribe the two people who worked the to-go counter to let me put my message in a sleeve and ensure it was on the cup of coffee Dr. Kuzma purchased. Subsequently, communication between us was established."

"What happened next?" Persik asked.

"I gave his name to the ambassador, who forwarded it to Jakarta. That's when I learned he was the world's leading scientist in active camouflage technology, which makes something invisible by blending it into the surroundings so that optical sensors, surveillance cameras, and other detection systems don't know it's there."

"The Minister said that with his technology a row of tanks on a battlefield could approach an enemy position unseen, or a person could walk into a room undetected and listen to a conversation," Wayan said.

"I don't understand how it works, but I was told by Jakarta that, even though many nations have built similar systems based on his published research before the Ukrainian government put a lid on his work, none have gotten past the Achilles' heel of motion, which negates the camouflage. Kuzma says that someone in his government must have told the Russians that he found a way around this, which is why they kidnaped him and his wife," Tjay explained. "This technology will significantly enhance our military and allow us to barter for sophisticated weaponry, money, and whatever else we want from the United States and other Western powers."

"The Minister also said," Eka segued, "that the doctor and his lab are going to be moved to a military base."

"Dr. Kuzma confirmed that move and wrote that it would happen a week from today when his new facilities at a military base are complete."

"Where is the military installation?" Persik asked.

"Kubinka Air Base is forty-five miles from here. As you might expect, security is tight, and once he'd there, we'll lose contact with him."

"Grabbing him before he's moved to the base is only half the problem because we were told he won't go without his wife," Eka interjected.

"Olena. The Russians are keeping her in a tiny one-room cabin in Oymyakon, under the watch of an FSB agent living in the cabin next to hers. As you said, Kuzma is adamant that he won't leave the country without her."

"Because she doesn't know us, convincing Olena that we're there to rescue her and that she's not being kidnapped a second time will be challenging," Eka said. "We know that getting her from Oymyakon to Moscow will be very difficult. However, without her cooperation, it'll be impossible."

"I agree," Persik added. "She might also believe that asking her to come with us is an FSB setup to justify sending her to a prison camp, the new name for what they once called a gulag. I'm sure they'd like to have her there now but know her husband would refuse to work if they sent her to one because of the high mortality rate within prison camps. But if she tried to escape Oymyakon, that might tip the scales."

"Any thoughts on how we convince her we're not FSB and to come with us?" Wayan asked.

Tjay thought for a moment before reaching into his pocket and removing several of the notes that Kuzma dropped by his table, handing them to Wayan. "Give these to her. She'll know his handwriting."

"The Minister said that you and your colleagues are very resourceful."

"He's being overly optimistic," Wayan replied. "One reason for this optimism may be that, in his words, we're nobodies. If we're caught or killed, the Indonesian government can deny being involved and make up any story about why we abducted, or tried to abduct, Olena Kuzma."

"All of you are the antithesis of nobodies and have a large set of bolas," Tjay replied, referring to the Indonesian equivalent of cojones. "The Minister of Defense is a cold and ruthless, but logical, sonofabitch. But he wouldn't have asked you to do this if he didn't believe you could get the her away from the FSB."

"I'm curious. Do you know why Kuzma wants to defect to Bali, not the United States, French Polynesia, or a similar location? That seems odd," Wayan said.

"He has it in his head that Bali is the Garden of Eden combining, he says, beauty and freedom. He says the Russian and Ukrainian governments have restricted his movements and kept him under constant watch, making him feel like a prisoner."

"We're going to do the same."

"But it'll be in the Garden of Eden."

"Assuming we get Olena out of Oymyakon and to Moscow, how does Fedir Kuzma get rescued when his guards seem to stick to him like glue?" Persik asked.

"The plan is for one of our embassy staff to create a diversion at the restaurant he and I frequent. In the ensuing chaos, I'll hustle him out the rear door and into a waiting vehicle while another of our embassy employees locks the door behind us from the outside. We already have that key. From the restaurant, Dr. Kuzma and I will go to our safehouse outside the city, taking a circuitous route where we know security cameras are absent. If your mission is successful, as I expect, you'll be waiting for us there with Olena," Tjay said.

"If we're both successful, that only leaves how to get the couple out of the country," Eka said.

"I'm open to all suggestions," Tjay replied after a sigh. "The Russians will tighten their border security and seal our embassy when they discover I've bolted out the back door of the restaurant with him. They may even seal entry before then once they learn three Indonesians have abducted his wife."

"If that's the hand we're dealt, we'll work with it. Can you get each of us an encrypted satphone and put in a number where we can reach you 24/7?" Wayan asked.

"Yes, but realize that the FSBs Service of Special Communications and Information branch, their equivalent of the NSA, is very good at breaking encryption. To complicate matters, the satphones won't work outside in the extreme cold where you're going because the circuitry will freeze."

"Noted. We'll also need sufficient rubles to bribe our way out of anything that might confront us," Wayan stated.

"I have a contingency fund."

"You'll need to get the phones and money to us quickly because we leave for Oymyakon at nine tomorrow morning."

"Where are you staying?"

Wayan told him.

"It's nice to know that Aeroflot is consistent," Persik said, squirming in his seat, which had the same degree of comfort as their other flight. He was sitting by the window with Eka Endah to his left and Gunter Wayan on the aisle.

"Only an hour and a half more," Eka reassured him, not having to mention that, after changing planes twice, they'd left Moscow ten and a half hours ago.

"Your admirer doesn't give up easily," Persik added, referring to the person in the aisle seat across from Wayan who made no secret of focusing on Eka's legs.

"I'm sure the only time they see someone like Eka is in a magazine with a trifold insert in the middle," Wayan added, that response getting him a sharp elbow to the ribs.

Wayan and Eka lived together in a large residence, which also served as their office, on the grounds of the Bulgari Resort in Bali; their stay comped because they proved who framed the resort owner for murder and, in the process, saved her life. Although they weren't married, they were a couple, and decided to take it slow and see where their relationship led.

When the aging Ilyushin turboprop landed at Ust Nera at four in the morning, seven hours ahead of Moscow time, the tour group was ushered into a waiting bus a dozen paces from the bottom of the deplaning stairway. The thirty-seat Pavloro 4234 was built in 2003 and retrofitted with an airline-style bathroom, which replaced six of those seats. It had the same cushy seating as the Ilyushin and, when it left the factory new, had a top speed of fifty-nine mph. Since then, age caught up with the deteriorating vehicle, and on a good day it might get to fifty mph—which was why it was on the Oymyakon runs where speed wasn't a consideration.

Although the drive from Ust Nera to Oymyakon was only two hundred sixty-six miles, it would take fourteen and a half hours to drive to the settlement, meaning the average speed of the bus was eighteen mph. This was due to a combination of the icy roads, primarily through the mountain passes, and because the Kolyma Highway had been chewed up over the years by heavy vehicles, which transported fuel and other essentials, limiting the speed of vehicles even in the best of weather conditions.

During their journey, the group was provided with three box lunches, each with two water bottles, a mystery-meat sandwich on brown bread, and a fruit cup. The drive took them across the Suntar, Agayakan, and Tireh-yuryakh rivers, stopping to refuel in Tomtor, a rare earth mining town of twelve hundred, nineteen miles from Oymyakon, which didn't have either a diesel or gas refueling station.

As the bus was being refueled, the tour guide handed out the canvas bags stacked in the rear seats, each stenciled with a tourist name. Inside were three layers of clothing. A Merino wool top, pants, and wool socks were the base layer. The insulating or middle layers, which could be removed if a person got too warm, consisted of warm trousers, a fleece vest, thick socks, and thin gloves. A waterproof parka, trousers, outer gloves, and fleece-lined neck buff was the final layer. Rubber boots, a balaclava, and protective creams for the face and lips completed the bag's contents. It took forty-five minutes for everyone to put on their clothing and apply the protective creams, after which the driver cut the heat to the inside of the bus so that no one would cook before they arrived at Oymyakon.

Before taking this trip, no one in the group had experienced below-freezing weather. Their first taste of it came in Moscow in aggregated thirty seconds when they boarded the bus at the airport to go to the hotel and on the return. The temperature at that time was fourteen degrees Fahrenheit. However, the weather at their destination would be fifty-four degrees colder.

"Everyone, make sure you apply the protective creams to your face and lips because, if bare skin is exposed to this extreme temperature, it'll freeze in two minutes, and you'll get frostbite in five," the tour guide admonished. "If that happens, expect little in the way of medical care. The nearest hospital is in Ust Nera, fourteen and a half hours behind us. The bus will depart at five tomorrow afternoon." With a nod from the guide, the driver opened the bus door and the sub-zero air rushed inside. It was seven-thirty pm.

As the tourists disembarked from the bus, the mayor and a handful of the settlement's residents were standing outside. The tour company pre-arranged each person's housing according to how many traveled together, such as couples, because some cabins were larger than others. The three non-tourists were the last off the bus and were staying in the five-room addition, with a separate entry door, that the enterprising resident built.

"This is it," their host said in broken English, the resident having been told that English was the preferred language of their guests since they didn't speak Russian. "Because you're from a warm climate, I set my heat at its maximum: sixty-eight degrees Fahrenheit. However, as it's particularly frigid this time of year, that temperature won't hold. You'll be lucky if it reaches fifty-two degrees."

"Good to know," Eka responded.

The interior of their cabin was stark. A table and six chairs were to the left of the entry door, in front of the small kitchen counter. Straight ahead at the far end of the addition were five doors, each leading to a bedroom that was just large enough for a cot and a space to lay a backpack or roller bag.

"There are two outhouses in the back. Both are unlit, so take that flashlight when you go," the resident said, pointing to it on the kitchen counter. "Because outside plumbing will freeze, I melt snow and ice on my stove to make drinking water. Yours is in the large metal pot on the counter. Scoop it out with the ladle and pour it into one of the metal cups. We cook by wood, and the stove is on my side, which has a separate entrance. I'll keep your water pot filled and set your food on the table three times a day."

"I'm surprised that you have electricity," Wayan said, seeing the LED bulbs that illuminated the cabin's interior.

"We have a coal and wood-fueled power plant that produces electricity for our basic needs, the most important of which is heat. We use wood-burning stoves for cooking because it reduces our power consumption, and getting replacement parts for electric appliances is difficult and expensive."

"Internet?" Eka asked.

"The satellite link is high-speed. However, word of caution. Don't use any electronic device outside because the battery and electrical components will become inoperative in five minutes."

"We heard that from our driver," Persik commented, subconsciously touching the satphone in his pocket.

"I noticed a man watching us from a distance as we got off the bus," Wayan said. "Forgive me for saying this, but he looked too young and trim to be a resident."

Their host laughed. "FSB. He and the woman in the cabin beside him, who he's guarding, arrived less than two months ago. The man isn't friendly, and we don't speak with him. He gets supplies delivered from Tomtor for himself and the woman, so he's not a drain on the resources of our settlement."

"Why did he come to meet our bus if he's guarding the woman?"

"He was going to tell the driver to take him to Tomtor tonight or tomorrow to get something he can't requisition from Moscow."

"Like what?" Persik asked.

"Vodka. He's done this before with other tour bus drivers."

"Where did you say his cabin was?" Eka asked.

"Two down," the host said, pointing to his left.

"And the woman? To the left or right of that?"

"To the left. She's three cabins down."

"One more question. When is sunrise?" Wayan asked.

"Approximately nine-fifty, and sunset is around three-thirty."

Once the host left to return to his side of the cabin, the non-tourists sat around the table to discuss how to rescue Olena Kuzma and drive the fourteen-plus hours on the single highway without being apprehended. And, if they made it that far, how to get to Moscow.

"Any thoughts on how we get Olena Kuzma away from her FSB handler and out of a place where locals don't own vehicles, and then get back to Moscow before they move her husband to the airbase in five days?" Wayan asked.

Everyone avoided eye contact with him except for Eka.

3

Olena Kuzma was doing what she did every day, which was reading a boring book taken from the stack given to her by the guard. All had the commonality of praising the Russian government and its leaders or predicting the eventual degradation and fall of the West. She knew this was a pile of rubbish because her country shared a border with the Russian Federation, and no Russian she spoke with believed that propaganda. However, believing and expressing that belief was different because the latter was likely to get a midnight visit from the FSB.

Olena relied on reading to maintain her sanity because she was prohibited from having a computer or a satphone. However, she got to speak to her husband once a week for fifteen minutes; that concession was made to the scientist in return for his willingness to continue his research in Moscow. The call was made using her guard's satphone, which he brought to her cabin every Monday evening, standing near to hear her side of the conversation and retrieve the phone at the end of the call.

When she first arrived, her guard would come unannounced to her cabin three times daily to ensure she hadn't fled. That made little sense to her. The settlement had no vehicles; if someone tried escaping on foot, they'd freeze to death long before reaching Tomtor, nineteen miles away. After the first week, the guard came to the same conclusion and cut his unannounced visits to once every two days, performing his last check this morning. Therefore, the knock on Olena's door surprised her, especially since residents didn't go out at night, preferring to socialize during the day when temperatures were twenty degrees warmer.

Expecting that it was the guard making another impromptu visit, she was shocked to see an unfamiliar face. Knowing about the tourists, she assumed the person standing in front of her was lost and seeking shelter. She let Eka inside and slammed the door shut behind her.

"Are you lost?" Olena asked in English, which she believed was a universal language.

"Not in the least. I and two others are here to take you to your husband," Eka answered, her voice quivering from the cold.

"Are you FSB?"

"I'm an Indonesian private investigator."

"Tell whoever's holding your leash at the FSB that they need to come up with a better story to get me to trust someone. Get out."

"It's true."

"I'm in an immense prison without bars, and my husband is so heavily guarded in Moscow that he couldn't communicate with a mouse without the FSB recording the conversation. Escape for both of us is impossible. Let me return to my boring book while you tell your handlers that you fell flat on your face trying to get me to commit suicide by following you outside in this weather."

Eka reached into her pocket, removed her husband's notes to Tjay, and handed them to her. She immediately recognized his writing and read them. When she finished, her demeanor changed, and she directed Eka to one of two chairs at the kitchen table.

"You said three of you are here to take me to my husband," Olena stated. "Are you part of the tour group which arrived this evening?"

"Yes."

"And you have a way to get me out of here?"

Eka said that she did.

"When do we leave?"

"Now," Eka answered, surprised with her fast response. "Grab warm clothes and whatever else you need and follow me."

Olena didn't need to be told twice and quickly gathered what she needed. Before they left, she ripped a page from her notebook, drew something on it, and placed it at the edge of the kitchen counter.

Operating a vehicle in the extreme cold requires a different mindset, knowing that at minus fifty degrees Fahrenheit, materials and fluids are adversely affected. The engine's oil gets thick and sticky, increasing the torque required to crank it; a car battery's effectiveness decreases and provides less torque to start the engine, tire pressure goes down, and a host of other anomalies also require attention. The three Indonesians and one Ukrainian were oblivious to these facts, ignorance becoming bliss because the town had an electrical cord for tourist buses, allowing the driver to keep the engine block warm so the vehicle would start on demand. In addition, the mayor had placed a hide tarp over the bus window, keeping ice off it.

As Wayan and Persik removed the tarp, they saw the engine block cable connected to a socket in the front grill. Neither knew what it was but pulled it from the socket, figuring they couldn't drive away with it attached. When they returned to the vehicle, Wayan started the bus, the heat and defrosting switches already at their maximum settings. Because there was only one highway, Wayan turned left onto it. It was 9:10 pm.

Because he had no previous winter driving experience, Wayan started out shaky, shifting the vehicle on the icy roads to gain speed as if he were in Bali. Even with chains, the bus came close to skidding off the icy highway twice. Following the second slide, Olena offered to take his place at the wheel, saying she was accustomed to driving in this type of weather.

"You won't get an argument from me," Persik said, with Eka agreeing.

Knowing he was in over his head, Wayan stopped the bus and switched places with Olena.

The change in the bus's stability was immediately noticeable, Olena holding it rock-steady, expertly adjusting her speed as she shifted to compensate for the tight turns and elevation changes. Along the way, two large trucks passed them, going in the opposite direction. Wayan surmised they were carrying goods to Tomtor because of the size of the vehicles and that the town was behind them.

Everything went smoothly for the next ten hours until it snowed, which was rare below zero degrees Fahrenheit because of a lack of moisture. However, in the area where they were driving, moist air was abundant, and as it rose and cooled, it produced snow. The amount of moisture meant they were in a severe snowstorm.

"This is fierce," Olena said, her wipers barely able to keep the snow off her windows so that she could see the road, which rapidly became obscured. When that happened, she focused on keeping the bus between the trees to her left and right, knowing that it was the road, even though she couldn't see it. "If this keeps up, the highway will be impassable and we'll get stuck, needing to wait for a plow to rescue us."

"I'm not sure rescue is the right word," Wayan corrected. "By that time, the FSB will be searching for us. Since we won't have transportation, we'll be easy to find and arrest."

"The alternative is that the snowplow operator doesn't come in time, and we freeze to death because we'll eventually run out of gas to heat the bus. I get it. We drive as fast as we can to get past this storm or die," Olena said.

At eleven am the morning after Olena Kuzma left with Wayan's team, her FSB thug went to the cabin in which the bus driver was staying, pounded on the door, and when the Oymyakon resident appeared, brusquely told him to have the driver meet him the bus. He didn't give Olena Kuzma a second thought, believing it was impossible to escape the town without a vehicle because of the brutal temperature. As a result, he was in denial when he looked at the spot where the bus should have been and, seeing it wasn't there, told himself that either the driver had moved it or left for Tomtor without him. However, both those beliefs evaporated when he saw the driver coming toward him with a look of concern in his eyes.

"Where's my bus?" the driver asked, his voice muffled by the balaclava.

"You tell me," the thug replied, his voice less muffled by the wool scarf that went across his face and wrapped around his neck.

The driver shrugged.

The thug didn't give a flip about the bus. All he cared about was if Olena Kuzma was still in Oymyakon because, if she weren't, this would become his permanent duty station. He took off at a run toward her cabin.

One problem encountered when running in cold weather was that blood vessels restricted to maintain the body's core temperature, reducing blood flow. The colder it was outside, the harder it was for the body to warm vital organs. Therefore, it shunted blood from a person's extremities to their organs to get this warmth. As a result, by the time the thug burst into Olena's cabin, he could barely move his arms, and his heart felt like it would explode. Collapsing to his knees, he looked around and saw that she wasn't in the tiny wooden structure. What he did focus on was a folded piece of paper propped against a bottle at the edge of the kitchen counter. Struggling to get to his feet, which felt like lead weights, he unfolded the paper. Instead of leaving a note, he saw she'd drawn a hand with the thumb sticking between the index and middle fingers. Known as a swish, it was the equivalent of extending the middle finger at someone.

General Viktor Lazarev was the director of the FSB, its headquarters within the yellow-bricked Lubyanka building in the Meshchansky District of Moscow. Appointed by the president of the Russian Federation, the sixty-five-year-old held the highest rank in use by the Russian military. He was six feet four inches tall, lean, had thinning gray hair, and unconsciously pursed his lips in a way that conveyed a perpetual sense of disapproval. Because the State empowered him to do whatever he wanted without consequence to maintain homeland security, he was the most feared person in Russia.

Lazarev's management style was one of objectivity. He didn't see shades of gray, only black or white. Words such as think, believe, and doubt were not part of his lexicon. He expected those who communicated with him, verbally or in writing, to take a position, be precise, and back up their information with facts. Those who did were promoted. Those who didn't were assigned to functions described by those within the organization as bureaucratic hell, meaning rote and monotonous administrative duties, or sent to remote locations and forgotten about. Therefore, before anyone sent something to him, they double-checked their facts.

Not wanting Oymyakon to be his permanent duty station and retirement home following Olena Kuzma's disappearance, the thug searched every cabin, the power plant, general store, and storage spaces within the settlement. Failing to find her, he methodically walked the surrounding area, looking for footprints in the snow or other evidence of her presence. There was none. Therefore, having no alternative, he reported her escape at one in the afternoon local time, which was six in the morning in Moscow.

The thug's supervisor, brought from his sleep by the phone call, became intensely alert with the shot of adrenalin that entered his bloodstream upon hearing of the escape. After asking a plethora of questions, most of which the thug couldn't answer, he ended the call and phoned his supervisor. And so it went until news of Olena Kuzma's disappearance reached Lazarev at eight am Moscow time.

Not only did the snow coming down on the aging bus not lessen, but it increased significantly and was accompanied by a strong wind perpendicular to the bus that threatened to tip it over. Conditions were close to a whiteout, meaning visibility was nonexistent. Olena slowed the bus to a crawl, barely able to see the treelines at the edges of the road. They were two-thirds of the way to Ust Nera, Eka keeping track of their position on her satphone, which operated efficiently within the warmth of the bus.

"If conditions worsen and this turns into a whiteout, it won't take long for the snow to get too deep for our vehicle to get through it, notwithstanding that I won't be able to see the trees to know if I'm on the road or going into the woods. We'll be forced to stop," Olena stated.

"We could call Tjay," Persik volunteered.

"Whatever help he sends won't get here before the FSB. Since there's only one highway in and out of Oymyakon, if we get stuck on this highway, they'll find us one way or another—alive if our fuel holds out and the heater keeps going and dead if not." Wayan added. "If we keep moving and by some miracle get past this storm, we continue with Eka's plan of chartering a plane in Ust Nera to take us to Moscow, hoping the FSB believes we're driving or taking a public mode of transport."

A minute later, Eka held up her satphone. "Look at this," she said, turning it toward Wayan and Persik. A red dot showed their position on a crooked blue line marked as the Kolyma Highway.

"You wanted to show us we're in the middle of nowhere?" Persik asked, looking at the screen.

"Look closer," she said, expanding the view with her fingers until the name Myaundzha, which was at the top of the screen, became more pronounced.

"Myaundzha?" Persik asked, not coming close to pronouncing it correctly.

"I think that's where the driver stopped to top off his fuel," she said. "Because the signs were in Russian, I didn't see Myaundzha, the English name for that settlement. However, I remember we arrived five hours after leaving Ust Nera."

"How far is that settlement from us?" Persik asked.

"It's hard to judge scale on this small screen, but it appears that we're almost on top of it."

Olena slammed on the brakes which, because everyone was standing, put them in a pile on the floor as the bus skidded and slid for thirty feet before stopping.

When they stood and looked out the driver's window, they didn't need to ask Olena for an explanation why she hit the brakes so hard. Ten feet ahead of them, a three feet high snowdrift blocked their way. If she'd been going only slightly faster, the bus would have crashed into it, destroying the front of it.

"What now?" Olena asked, making a general comment rather than expecting an answer.

That fact was lost on Persik, who vented his frustration. "Let me take a stab at answering," he said. "We can't go forward because of the snowdrift, and we can't go back because we'll probably run into the FSB, which I'm sure are sending a bunch of people down this highway after us. If we remain here, we'll stay alive only as long as we have fuel to keep us warm, or are captured. Have I got this right?"

"Spot on," Wayan answered.

"I'm not one to throw a rock at a glass house, but I can't count the number of situations you've dragged me into that I didn't come within a hair of dying," he said, looking at Wayan.

Eka, who was standing beside Olena, patted her on the arm. "Don't take them too seriously. They occasionally go through this. I'm not sure if it's male bonding, an expression of camaraderie, or bromance."

"To set the record straight," Wayan said, "we're here because you volunteered Eka and my services to the Minister of Defense, and he told you to accompany us. As for the other situations, you may have a point."

4

The Pavloro 4234 quickly became surrounded by snow so deep that, even without the drift, the bus couldn't move. Although everyone was warm, because the vehicle had plenty of fuel, they were literally stuck in the middle of nowhere and an unknown distance from Myaundzha. Their situation was finite because, when the fuel tank ran dry, they'd freeze in the extreme cold.

"Now would be a good time to call Tjay and ask for help although," Persik said, "given where we are, it may not arrive in time."

"It's worth a try," Wayan said, removing the satphone from his pocket. As he did, two pinpricks of light pierced the fiercely blowing snow.

"We've got company," Wayan said, everyone focused on the approaching lights, which gradually became brighter.

Because of the wind, there was no sound until a minute later, when a huge snowplow burst through the drift in front of them and suddenly stopped feet from the bus.

"That was close," Olena said, breathing heavily from the shock of the near impact.

"Close, but lucky," Wayan added. "He might have cleared the path ahead."

"Even if he did," Olena volunteered, "if the snow is falling hard on the way to Ust Nera, we'll get stuck again and may not be as lucky having another plow stumble on us," she said. "Since I speak Russian, let me talk with the driver and see what he can tell us," she said before putting on her coat, hat, scarf, and gloves.

They watched as she pulled a lever, opening the bus door inward, and she jumped into the waist-deep snow, Wayan closing the door behind her. Olena trudged through the heavy snow until she reached the passenger side of the plow, after which the door swung open and she stepped up into the cab of the vehicle.

Ten minutes later, she returned and Wayan opened the door.

"The driver is from Myaundzha, a town of fifteen hundred that's half a mile in front of us. His company has a contract to clear the section of the Kolyma Highway we're on. He's offered to pull us out of the snow and plow ahead of us to ensure we get there. He said fuel station has a café that's open 24/7 and we can get something to eat."

"What are we waiting for, I'm hungry," Persik said, drawing laughs.

After attaching chains to both the blow and the bus, the snowplow driver backed up his vehicle and pulled the bus onto the section of road he'd just cleared. Although the heavy snowfall continued, getting to Myaundzha was a breeze because they were following the four-ton truck. When they arrived, Wayan asked Olena to invite the driver to join them by saying they wanted to reward him for his trouble.

The café wasn't a traditional diner. Instead, it was the rear of someone's home in which four Formica-topped tables and aging wooden chairs had been placed. The chime that sounded when opening the door alerted those in the house, and a man appeared several minutes later. Although he didn't speak English, he understood the word coffee and how many they wanted when Wayan held up five fingers, including the driver in the count. While waiting, he and Persik brought two tables together and assembled the chairs around them. The driver entered several minutes later as the homeowner returned with five cups and a large pot of coffee.

"Is there a menu?" Wayan asked.

Olena translated for the homeowner.

He and the driver laughed.

"He says all he has is today's special, which is Stroganina, Indigirka salad, and for dessert, Kyorchekh."

"I have no idea what any of those are but tell him to bring enough for everyone."

After the man left, the driver spoke with Olena. From his hand gestures, he was explaining something to her.

"He says the café serves the same three items every day and that the menu never varies," Olena translated.

"What did we order?" Wayan asked.

She asked the driver, who told her.

"Stroganina is made from thin slices of frozen fish. The main ingredient in Indigirka Salad is diced pieces of frozen fish."

"The first two courses are frozen fish and frozen fish," Persik summarized. "And for dessert?"

"Cow's milk, berries, and sour cream."

"That's a winner," he said.

Because none of the dishes were cooked, and keeping something frozen in the permafrost conditions of Siberia was easy, the homeowner returned in five minutes and laid out two platters of food, going into the kitchen twice again to retrieve the silverware and desert.

Everyone started putting food on their plates and began eating. As the platters emptied, Wayan told Olena to have the homeowner bring another round of food, which again arrived in less than five minutes. It was also quickly devoured.

"All joking aside, this food was amazing," Persik said, after finishing the last of the Kyorchekh on his plate.

The homeowner took the plates and platers back into the kitchen and, after setting another pot of coffee on the table, left.

"Tell the driver that we appreciate his help and give him this," Wayan said to Olena, sliding the thirty thousand rubles he removed from his pocket to her, the equivalent of five hundred US dollars and the average monthly income for someone living in Siberia.

The driver's eyes widened as Olena translated and handed him the money, quickly putting it in the pocket of his parka before the owner returned.

"Tell him we're prepared to be more generous if he can drive us to Ust Nera because our bus can't handle these road conditions," Wayan stated.

She translated.

"The driver said these heavy storms are common and usually last ten to twelve hours making the highway impassable until midday to all but his snowplow."

"Okay, but can he get us to Ust Nera?"

Olena asked, the driver replying that, for the right price, he'd be willing to take them there in his snowplow.

"The next question," Wayan asked, "is how we keep from freezing because there's not enough room in the driver's cab for everyone."

Olena asked, the response being that he'd ensure that whoever rode in the truck bed would be warm but uncomfortable during the five hour journey.

Wayan, who knew he had no other way to get to Ust Nera, reached into his backpack and pulled out ten packets of rubles, each the equivalent of a thousand US dollars. Dividing the stack, he slid half to the driver, who was sitting across from him. The driver wasted no time, greedily grabbing the packets and stuffing it into his pockets.

"Tell him that he'll get the other half when we get to Ust Nera," Wayan said.

Olena told him, the two conversing for a minute before he went outside.

"He's going to refuel the truck and get a few items he needs from his house."

"I guess we'll find out what warm but uncomfortable means when he returns," Wayan stated, "because warm for someone living here might mean something completely different than it would for someone living in Bali."

He was right.

The driver's snowplow was a modified dump truck that was twenty-four feet long, eight and a half feet wide, ten and a half feet high, and had an empty weight of seven tons, with the ten-feet-wide plow on the front adding another ton. When the driver pulled it in front of the café, Olena and Eka got into the front cab, while Wayan and Persik climbed into the truck bed. In the back were two large reindeer pelts and two heaters, each attached to a twenty pound propane tank, capable of providing heat for ten hours. Once they started the heaters and confirmed they were working, the driver got underway.

The high sides of the truck's beds kept the wind off them and, combined with the cold weather gear they wore, the reindeer fur kept them semi-warm. The driver's statement that they'd be uncomfortable was as advertised. The vehicle's shocks and struts were worn to the point of being nearly non-functional, causing the vehicle to tip to the left and sway and bounce at highway speed, giving Wayan and Persik numerous bruises on their lower body as it slammed onto the steel truck bed. The beating continued unabated until seven-thirty in the morning Moscow time, when the driver pulled into the Ust Nera train station.

The two men were slow getting out of the truck bed, requiring the driver's help to get them onto the pavement. Both walked unsteadily around the truck a couple of times to simulate circulation in their lower body. Once their balance returned,

Wayan reached into his pocket and gave the driver the remaining half of his payment.

"I'll need his services a while longer," Wayan told Olena, who asked the driver, receiving an enthusiastic nod in return.

"Tell him to wait here while the rest of us go into the terminal."

As the driver returned to the cab of his vehicle, they went into the warm building,

"Olena, you're accompanying Eka and I to the ticket counter and purchase four tickets to Moscow. You'll be using Eka's credit card to make that purchase."

"Why my card?" Eka asked.

"Because my card is at its limit and yours always works."

"Should I ask why we're taking a train and not flying?"

"When the FSB comes looking for us, which we know they will, I want them to believe we're on a train."

"Not bad, Wayan."

After purchasing the tickets for the five pm train, they returned to the truck and had the driver to take them to airport, a ten minute drive. The plan was to charter a jet to take them to Moscow, thereby avoiding the commercial airport's ID and security checks since it was a domestic flight.

The airport consisted of one building which had a decrepit prop plane salvaged from a crash sitting next to the entrance. Wayan, Eka, and Olena went inside and saw that the single check-in counter belonged to Yakutia Airlines, the same one which flew them into the Ust Nera thirty-five hours earlier. There was no charter airline or general aviation desk. That there was only one airline and no other air service for the town never occurred to Wayan and Eka because the tour group never entered the building. Instead, they were ushered down a stairway and into a waiting bus. With their plan for getting Olena to Moscow no longer possible, they left the building and rejoined Persik and the driver.

"Any ideas?" Wayan asked after he explained the situation to Persik.

Persik shook their head. The driver, who didn't understand English, asked Olena why everyone looked so sullen. She told him.

"If you have the money, charter a plane," he told her.

"There's no charter company."

"This is Russia. Everything has a price. Go to the Yakutia desk agent, tell them you and your friends want to charter a direct flight to Moscow, and offer to pay them and the aircrew the going rate."

"Which is?"

"Whatever you agree upon, not including a generous fee for your driver who made the suggestion," he replied with a smile. "If you reach an agreement, they'll cancel the scheduled flight and you're on your way."

"It can't be that simple," Persik said. "You can't cancel a scheduled flight and make it a charter."

"This is Russia," the driver repeated. "If you have the money, nothing is impossible."

"It's our only option," Wayan said. "Olena, let's go back into the building and give it a try." They entered at three pm local time, which was eight am in Moscow.

"Why am I getting this information so late?" Lazarev asked his aide, who'd just informed him that Olena Kuzma had escaped from Oymyakon with the help of three Indonesian tourists. "By the account of that idiot assigned to guard her, it's believed she left eighteen hours ago."

"Her handler," his aide said, skirting by the moniker of idiot, "just discovered she was missing," the aide replied, not mentioning that part of the delay was because of the over-cautiousness of his staff.

"Who are these tourists?"

The aide gave him a folder containing the visa applications, which had their photos attached.

"A police detective and a former police detective and his partner who own an investigation agency in Bali."

"An unlikely group to abduct Olena Kuzma," the aide said.

"Yet one I would have selected because, when applying for a visa, coming as part of a tour would seem benign."

The aide shut up.

"How is it possible these three knew Olena Kuzma's location?"

The aide was about to respond that he didn't know when the general held up his right hand, preventing him from answering.

"Very few knew that she was taken to Oymyakon. Someone talked—an issue we can address later. The better question is why rescue her since her husband is the genius behind active camouflage technology? Her value to us is only so that he'll be motivated to continue his research."

"Maybe the Indonesians feel they can disrupt that cooperation."

"To what end? That belief holds significance if the United States, China, or another global military power took her. But Indonesia? There's something we're missing."

The general thought for several minutes before continuing. "Taking Olena Kuzma only makes sense if they also plan to rescue her husband, because they know she won't leave the country without him, or they plan to disrupt his work knowing he won't cooperate with us if he can't speak to his wife and confirm her safety. The still doesn't answer the question of why Indonesia is involved."

"Doctor Kuzma is under heavy guard in the center of Moscow. I can't see how they can effect his rescue."

"And yet they took Olena Kuzma from Oymyakon—something that I believed was impossible. Don't underestimate the tourists. They have good intelligence, resources, and have demonstrated they're cunningly creative. If they worked for me, I'd pin a metal on them. Instead, I'll have to torture them to find out what they know before killing them. When will Kuzma be taken to Kubinka Airbase?"

"In four days, when his lab is finished."

"Colonel Assonov's special forces team is assigned to that airbase. Have him ensure everything is ready for Doctor Kuzma's arrival no later than tomorrow morning and ensure a squad of his men guard the doctor at that time until then. I'm not waiting four days."

The aide acknowledged the order. "He's due to speak with his wife tomorrow," the aide added.

"There's going to be a technical problem," he irritably replied. "Getting back to Olena Kuzma's escape, we know that they stole the tourist bus eighteen hours ago. There's only one road out of Oymyakon, and that ends in Ust Nera."

The general began typing on his keyboard, returning his attention to the aide two minutes later.

"Interestingly, if the weather report on my screen is correct, there was eight to ten inches of snow with wind gusting to thirty miles an hour on the upper third of the Kolyma Highway during that time. Only a plow could get through that, meaning they may not have reached Ust Nera and are stuck on the highway. Have an army battalion work their way down that highway toward Oymyakon, beginning in Ust Nera and send our agents to Ust Nera's to check the airport and train station, showing pictures of the four and asking if anyone has seen them. If the army doesn't find them on the Kolyma Highway, the only place they could be is in that town."

The aide went to his office and called the Western Siberian Military District headquarters in Novosibirsk, relaying Lazarev's order to send troops to search the Kolyma Highway, from Ust Nera to Oymyakon, to search for four fugitives whose photos he forwarded. The aide next called the closest FSB field office to Ust Nera, a map showing it was in Yakutsk. Speaking with the head of that office, Colonel Stasik Nazarov, he repeated Lazarev's order and left it up to him on how to carry it out.

5

The Yakutia Airlines agent sitting at the counter doing paperwork was a woman in her mid-fifties, with gray hair, piercing dark brown eyes, and wearing the airline's winter uniform of a dark blue jacket over a skirt that ended just above the knees. No one was near the counter when Olena and Wayan approached, the next flight being four hours away.

"Excuse me, can I see the manager?" Olena asked. "We need to charter a plane."

"I'm the manager, and we have no aircraft for charter."

And the negotiations began. Olena and the woman spoke in an amiable tone, their discussion lasting ten minutes while Wayan silently watched.

"She'll do it for a price," Olena said. "But the only aircraft available is the Antonov AN-140 parked outside. She says it has a range of twenty-two hundred miles and a maximum speed of three hundred fifty mph. The problem, as she pointed out, is that Moscow is a thousand miles further, meaning we'll have to refuel en route."

"How much does she want?"

"She says this aircraft's charter rate is four thousand dollars an hour. At max speed, I calculate it'll take us nine hours to reach Moscow."

"If we add an hour for an interim landing, refueling, and takeoff," Wayan said, "that's forty thousand dollars."

"Not quite. That's what the airline gets. That doesn't include the accommodation fee for her, the pilots, and the flight attendant."

"It seems like the hourly rate should include everything," Wayan said.

Olena asked.

"She explained that their fee is for ignoring the government rule on asking for identification and recording the identity of the person chartering the aircraft and the names of the passengers onboard. It also includes canceling the commercial flight for which this aircraft was scheduled with the excuse it needs to go to Moscow for maintenance."

"How does canceling a flight for maintenance and having it fly over three thousand miles make sense?"

"That's her problem," Olena volunteered.

"Okay. How much do she and the crew want? I have roughly forty thousand dollars in rubles left in my backpack."

"The amount is yet to be negotiated."

"Find out," Wayan stated.

She asked, coming back with an answer of twenty thousand dollars.

"Tell her I'll pay thirty-five thousand now and the balance when we reach Moscow. That's reasonable considering we won't know the exact flying time until we land. She and the crew can take their accommodation fee from my initial payment, and the airline gets the remaining twenty-five thousand when we land in Moscow."

Olena presented Wayan's idea, with the manager readily accepting.

The twin-engine turboprop took off at nine am. As it was taxiing, the manager placed a sign on her counter indicating that the last flight of the day was canceled and that passengers would be put on the next flight, which would depart at ten the following morning. She then left the building and returned home.

The FSB had seventy field offices, the nearest to Ust Nera being in Yakutsk, which was four hundred fifty miles to the northeast and the same field office from which Olena Kuzma's former guard came. Although Yakutsk had a sizeable civilian airport, government and military aircraft were stationed at the Magan airport. The FSB used the smaller facility seven and a half miles outside the city because it offered operational concealment for arriving and departing military flights.

The head of that field office was Colonel Stasik Nazarov. He was five feet nine inches tall, with short black hair and teeth slightly crooked and yellowed from neglect. His hands were calloused from not using gloves during his daily weightlifting workout. The physically fit colonel had a solid physique with a thick neck, bulging biceps, and the tree trunk legs associated with powerlifters.

Because the orders to go to Ust Nera came from General Lazarev, and Nazarov didn't want a second screwup, the first being one of his agents letting Olena Kuzma escape, he decided to lead the team and take five agents with him. Before leaving the field office, he assembled the agents in the conference room and discussed the possible ways the fugitives could leave the town. The consensus was that taking a commercial flight was the fastest and most plausible. Taking a train was the second, and driving across Siberia was a distant third. Therefore, their initial focus would be on the airport.

Once the meeting was finished, each agent grabbed their travel bag, which they were required to keep at the field office, and drove to Magan. They boarded the government turboprop an hour and twenty minutes after sunset at four-fifty in the evening, an hour behind local time in Ust Nera. They arrived at their destination seventy minutes later.

The security guard at the Ust Nera Airport had consumed the better part of a bottle of vodka when a turboprop landed and taxied to the terminal. The guard, who heard the aircraft land but could only see its outline from a distance, got a better look as it taxied into the lighted area and parked to the left of the terminal. The lack of insignias and that it landed unannounced indicated it belonged to the government and that whoever was onboard didn't want to advertise their presence.

Surprise arrivals by unmarked aircraft weren't uncommon in Ust Nera because the military liked to use their runway for pilots to practice their short-field takeoffs and landings, or crashes and dashes, as the pilots called them. Occasionally, they'd stop and taxi to the terminal for a restroom break or stretch their legs. Therefore, to the guard, this seemed like one of those flights.

After returning the bottle to his duffle bag, he started toward the aircraft to inspect the national ID cards and record the names of the six civilian men who disembarked because that was part of his job. However, the military was exempt from this requirement. As the guard approached the civilian leading the group, Nazarov showed his FSB creds, evaporating whatever thought the guard had of asserting his authority.

"You never saw this aircraft, nor us," Nazarov stated.

The guard didn't respond, only shaking his head several times in the affirmative.

"I want to look inside the terminal," he continued and, without waiting for an acknowledgment, took off briskly toward it, followed closely by his men.

The guard knew that arguing with the FSB, especially one with the rank of colonel, would get him a prison number stenciled to the back of his shirt. He ran ahead of the agents to the main entrance of the building, pulled the keys from his pocket as he did, and unlocked the door.

Once inside, the six agents thoroughly inspected the building, confirming it was empty. During their search, Nazarov saw the sign the manager placed on the Yakutia Airlines counter rescheduling the canceled flight to the following day. "Did the airline provide lodging for these passengers?" he asked the guard.

"The airline doesn't provide lodging for canceled flights. Passengers either return home or go to one of the two accommodations in town—the Solnechnaya Inn or Borkut Tourist Complex."

Nazarov saw the car rental stations to the right of the Yakutia Airlines counter, telling three of his men to take a set of keys from Hertz and check the inn and tourist complex. The guard told them how to get to both places.

Once his men left, the colonel asked how to get to the train station.

The guard explained how to get there.

Without further conversation, Nazarov took a set of keys and drove to the station with the two agents who remained with him. Inside, a dozen people were waiting for the next train to arrive in two hours. He presented his creds to the person behind the ticket counter, who was also the manager.

"Have you seen any of these people?" he asked without preamble, showing her four photos.

The woman said that she hadn't. "My shift started an hour ago; perhaps they took an earlier train."

"How many trains come through here in a day?"

"Four."

"Do you have the video from those cameras?" he asked, pointing to the security cameras in the corners of the terminal.

"They haven't worked in years, and repairing them is not in our budget."

Nazarov didn't ask if she had the names of passengers who previously purchased tickets because recording the names of train and bus passengers weren't required by law. Nazarov, who'd run into this problem before, asked another question that might give him the answers he was seeking.

"Did anyone use a credit card?" he asked.

"Almost everyone pays in cash but let me check since we haven't batched our credit card transactions."

Batching referred to processing credit card transactions at the close of the business day or at a time determined by the credit card processor.

It took only a minute to find what Nazarov requested.

"I have seven credit card receipts," the manager said, handing them to him.

Nazarov saw that Eka Endah had purchased six one-way tickets to Moscow's Leningradsky Railway Station.

"When does this train arrive in Moscow?" he asked, showing her the receipt.

"In two days and twenty and a half hours," she answered, knowing the train left the station nine and half hours ago and subtracting that time from the seventy-eight-hour journey.

"How many stops will it make before Moscow?"

"Twenty-five."

"Where are they?"

The manager took him to a railway chart on the wall that showed the train's route and stops.

"I'm not familiar with most of these towns."

"They're in rural areas that lack airports," she responded. "In the winter, most of their supplies come by rail, and because the roads in those areas are impassable this time of year, the train is their only travel option."

Removing the cell phone from his jacket pocket, he called Lazarev and told him what he'd learned, letting him decide whether to intercept the train before reaching Moscow, which he called option one, or apprehend the fugitives when they got to the Leningradsky Railway Station, which was option two.

"I don't want to arrest the three foreigners and Olena Kuzma at the Moscow train station. It's crowded, and there's always a large number of foreigners there. The commotion and publicity of your arresting them will be recorded on numerous cell phone cameras, making it difficult to hide their identities and suppress what happened. Therefore, option one." After conveying his decision, Lazarev ordered the FSB colonel to remain in Ust Nera until the interdiction of the fugitives was confirmed.

When the call with Nazarov ended, Lazarev's aide suggested they abort the military flights to Ust Nera. "Now that we know the fugitives are on the train, they're unnecessary," the aide concluded.

"Are they? A ticket is an indication expressing an intent. Because the station's surveillance cameras are inoperative, there's no way to know that they got on the train. Until I have that verification, I'm assuming they're either in Ust Nera or on their way there. And if they are on that train, they aren't going anywhere for several days, giving me time to intercept it before reaching Moscow."

Lazarev turned his attention to his computer screen, which showed weather predictions for the Kolyma Highway but not the previous weather. Picking up his phone and putting the call on speaker so his aide could hear, he asked the operator to connect him with the director of the government's meteorology office. When he came on the line, Lazarev asked what the weather was like on the Kolyma Highway between Oymyakon and Ust Nera for the previous twelve hours.

"There was heavy snowfall and intermittent whiteout conditions," the Kremlin's weather czar stated after accessing his computer.

"Could a bus have driven through that much snow?"

"That's highly unlikely. I have a list of trucks and semis that became stranded on the Kolyma Highway during that time. But I have no record of a bus. The only vehicles that are unaffected are snowplows, which we have under contract to clear stretches of that highway," the weather czar said.

When the general ended the call, he turned to his aide. "If the bus wasn't stranded, they may have reached Ust Nera and taken the train before the highway became impassable. They're also possibly in one of the small towns along that road."

"As you said, if they're on the train, they're stuck on it for three days. If they're in Ust Nera or one of the small towns along the highway, the military will find them."

"I wish I had your optimism because these three Indonesians have been very resourceful," Lazarev said, leaning back in his chair and trying to think what he'd do if in their position.

Three hours after receiving the call from Lazarev, troops and equipment from the Western Siberian Military District headquarters in Novosibirsk were brought onboard two Ilyushin IL-76 cargo aircraft stationed at the Tolmachevo Airport, which was ten miles from the center of the city. One aircraft carried three GAZ 23304 Tigers, an unarmored five-door vehicle, while the other transported a snowplow and twenty troops with their equipment. The IL-76, Russia's equivalent of the United States' C-17 Globemaster, had a massive interior and could land in as little as twenty-three hundred feet—a necessity because the length of Ust Nera's runway was only thirty-six hundred feet. Once airborne, the Ilyushins would take four hours to travel the twenty-one hundred miles, scheduled to land at eleven in the evening local time.

6

An hour after Nazarov told Lazarev that he believed the fugitives were on a train to Moscow, and ninety minutes before the two Ilyushins landed in Ust Nera, the Yakutia Airlines AN-140 was descending for its scheduled fuel stop at the Omsk Tsentralny Airport, which was halfway to Moscow. Wayan was asleep when the flight attendant woke him and said he was needed in the cockpit. Although the plane was shaking from turbulence, neither he nor the other fugitives noticed, having fallen asleep as soon as the aircraft left Ust Nera, exhausted from a previous lack of rest and the stress of their ordeal.

When he entered the cockpit, the pilot told the co-pilot he had the controls and waved Wayan forward. Because the turbulence was getting worse, Wayan knelt on the deck and grabbed the back of his seat with his left hand. Although neither was fluent in English, each knew enough to communicate.

"We're in the middle of a major snowstorm with gusts approaching thirty mph," the pilot said. "The storm is already over the Omsk airport, and approach control has advised that we're the last aircraft they'll vector to it because the weather is deteriorating so rapidly they expect to close it."

"What happens if the weather deteriorates faster than expected and the airport closes before we land?"

"By regulation, I must divert to my alternate airport, which I've been told by approach control will soon close when this storm passes over it."

"And if it does?"

"This storm is so large and is moving so quickly that I don't have a second alternate."

"You're saying that Omsk is our best and possibly the only place we can land."

"Yes. The airport is still above the minimum landing threshold, and I'll begin my approach in less than a minute. Expect severe turbulence as we descend because of the gusts and shifting winds. Because of this, I'll be landing with authority."

"I'm not familiar with that term," Wayan said.

"It means the landing will be very firm, and everyone is going to find out whether they have hemorrhoids," the pilot answered with a smile, appearing not stressed in the least.

Wayan, seeing the lack of fear on his face, relaxed.

"I'll also be carrying more speed than usual when I set down, so I'll hit the brakes aggressively to stop the aircraft," the pilot continued. "The flight attendant is telling your friends to strap in tight."

"What happens if the tower tells you the airport is closed as you're on the approach? Will you divert to the alternate airport?" Wayan asked.

"The radios have always been a problem on this aircraft. I'm setting this plane down."

The flight attendant and the four fugitives tightly strapped themselves into their seats, preparing for the descent. It was four-thirty pm in Omsk, three hours ahead of Moscow.

As the AN-140 approached the Omsk Tsentralny *Airport*, it bucked as if strapped to the back of a rodeo bull, resulting in the overhead bins opening as the plane descended. Using instruments, because there was nothing to see outside other than white swirling snow, the pilot locked onto the instrument landing system signal or ILS. This precision approach radar guided the aircraft to within two hundred feet of the ground. If the pilot couldn't see the runway then, he was required to execute a missed approach and give it another try or go to an alternate airport, which this pilot wasn't about to do.

The severe turbulence continued unabated as the plane lessened the steepness of its descent and slowed. The first hint that the aircraft was close to landing was a whirring sound from the flaps extending to increase the wingspan. That was followed by a bang denoting the landing gear had dropped into place. Seconds later, the aircraft slammed onto the runway, and the pilot hit the brakes hard, everyone's seatbelts straining to keep them in their seats. The plane continued to slow and, a minute later, parked in front of the VIP terminal.

As the pilot left the cockpit to lower the stairway, the four fugitives came forward and congratulated him on the landing.

"Did they close the airport?" Wayan asked.

"I don't know, I had radio problems," he replied, smiling.

"How long before the storm subsides, and we can continue to Moscow?" Wayan asked.

"It appears the radios are working again; let me check," the pilot said, calling the tower.

The discussion between the pilot and the tower lasted a minute. "The tower said the storm is projected to last until late tomorrow morning or early afternoon, after which it will take several hours to clear the runways and taxiways and de-ice aircraft so they can depart."

"We're looking at the better part of a day," Wayan said, confirming what he'd heard.

"A little longer. This isn't Moscow. I've been stuck here before, and it always takes them longer than they say because their snow removal equipment belongs in a museum, and if it doesn't break down, it moves with the speed of an arthritic pensioner. I'll speak with the VIP hostess, and they'll get us rooms for the night." The pilot then lowered the stairway, sucking the cold air and blowing snow into the plane.

The fugitives patted him on the back as they descended, holding onto the rails to keep from being thrown down the slippery stairs by the powerful gusts of wind. At the bottom, they stepped into three inches of new snow, trudging through it and working their way into the VIP terminal. Inside, a young woman was seated behind a counter. Seeing the Yakutia Airlines plane, she waved them inside.

The four fugitives walked to a grouping of chairs where the hostess couldn't hear and sat down.

"It sounds like we're stuck in Omsk until at least late afternoon tomorrow," Eka said, overhearing with Persik and Olena what the pilot told Wayan.

"The FSB, or whoever else the Russians send after us, will find us here before long," Persik stated. "There's only a couple of ways out of Ust Nera, and when they discover we're not on the train, they'll figure out we chartered this plane if they haven't already."

"If there's a train station nearby, we can go by rail to Moscow," Eka volunteered. "This snow may affect flying, but not a train."

Olena stepped forward. "She's right. It takes feet and not inches of snow to stop a train because there's so much weight on the wheels," she said. "I've taken a train in far worse conditions than this."

As Wayan and Olena went to speak to the hostess about the train schedule, the pilot, co-pilot, and flight attendant entered, waved to the hostess without stopping, and continued to the coffee cart in the back to warm up.

"Can you ask the hostess how far the train station is from here?" Wayan asked Olena.

"She says the Omsk-Passazhirsky train station is three miles away," Olena translated.

"Can she tell us when the next train leaves for Moscow?" Olena asked, and the hostess called the station.

"Two trains depart for Moscow every day," Olena said. "The next one leaves in three hours. Because we're fourteen hundred miles from Moscow, each makes many stops and has significant layovers, taking forty-three hours to reach Moscow."

Wayan and Olena went to where Persik and Eka were standing, out of hearing distance from the hostess. "Two days of exposure on a slow-moving train with the FSB searching for us is an eternity, and we'd be sitting ducks. They could board and look for us at any stop along our route. We'd be better off waiting for the storm to clear and continuing on our plane onto Moscow," Wayan said.

"Except, according to the timeline given by the pilot, we're equally vulnerable here," Persik added.

The hostess, seeing the looks on their faces with the discussion they were having, summoned Olena. The two spoke for several minutes before she returned.

"She said we have another option. While commercial aircraft can't take off and land, private pilots don't have that restriction if there's no instrument flight plan. She also said this airport has bush pilots who fly skiplanes in weather like this to transport supplies, mail, and people to remote sites that don't have a train or commercial airline service. They're considered private pilots."

"And she knows how to get in touch with them?" Persik asked.

"The hostess said they use a hangar on the opposite side of the airport, which has a snow strip runway behind it. In the winter, she said that it's the busiest spot at the airport and, for the right price, they'll fly anyone or anything, no questions asked, as long as where they're going has snow on the ground so that they can land."

"They're smugglers," Persik said.

"The four of us aren't exactly going down the centerline of legality," Wayan responded.

"Good point."

"What do you think?" Eka asked Wayan.

"That we're going to need more money from Tjay."

The hostess arranged for a truck to take them to the skiplane hangar. They approached the first person they saw, the pilot introducing himself as Kirill Belevich. He was five feet ten inches tall with short black hair, a slim physique, and a long stubble beard. The aircraft behind him was a bright yellow Cessna 207 skiplane thirty-two feet in length, nine feet seven inches in height, and a wingspan of almost thirty-six feet. It was designed to carry a maximum of seven passengers and had a service ceiling of thirteen thousand feet and a top speed of one hundred eighty-five mph.

"The hostess at the lounge told us we could hire a plane to get us out of Omsk," Wayan said.

"If the money is right."

"She also implied that you weren't particular about the people you take."

"If the money is right. I fly legal and illegal cargo and people, as do most of us in this hangar. Since you appear to be in a hurry to leave, I take it that someone is after you."

"You could say that."

"Who?"

"The FSB and possibly others in the government that we don't know about."

"That's good."

"Why is that good?" Eka asked with a note of skepticism.

"Because it increases my price. Where do you want to go?"

"Moscow," Wayan answered.

"Moscow is five hundred miles beyond the range of my aircraft. I'll need to refuel."

"Have you flown there before?" Persik asked.

"Probably a hundred times, and to neighboring Finland, an equal number. They're lucrative markets for smugglers."

It surprised Wayan that Belevich didn't have an issue discussing his illegalities with four people being chased by the FSB.

"How do you avoid being caught?" Eka asked.

"I fly nap-of-the-earth."

"Nap-of-the-earth?"

"Just above the trees."

"So that you're below radar," Persik concluded.

"Nap-of-the-earth," Belevich repeated.

"How long is the flight to Moscow?" Eka asked.

"A little over eight hours."

"And how much will this adventure cost?" Wayan asked. Belevich told him.

"We don't have the cash on us. Can we wire the funds?"

"As long as I receive them before you board my plane."

"Give me the numbers," Wayan said.

The pilot gave him the wiring instructions and account number for his offshore account, indicating that he and the other bush pilots had foreign bank accounts and only used domestic banks for their legitimate cargo.

"I'll be a second," Wayan said, walking away and calling Tjay, saying they'd been successful and that everyone was safe and coming home. However, they'd need additional funds wired to an offshore bank."

"Tell me how much and where," he said, not questioning the amount or why it was needed.

Wayan gave it to him and ended the call.

The funds were wired within minutes, and once Belevich verified the money was in his account, everyone boarded the Cessna. The aircraft lifted off the snow strip at six-thirty in the evening local time, which was three-thirty in the afternoon in Moscow.

7

The two Ilyushin military aircraft landed in Ust Nera at eleven pm local time. The unit's commander, Lieutenant Colonel Aleksandr Durchenko, was neither thin nor fat, stood five feet ten inches tall, had close-cropped black hair, and spoke in a deliberative voice devoid of humor that indicated he meant what he was saying. This unremarkable appearance was accentuated by two deep parallel shrapnel scars on the right side of his face from a bomb that exploded near him in Syria, only surviving because the person to his right bore the brunt of the blast.

The guard, who had returned to his security shack, saw the aircraft with military markings land and taxi to the terminal, squeezing into the remaining tarmac beside Nazarov's aircraft. Not wanting to get involved in whatever was happening, especially when the FSB and military were involved, he stayed in his shack.

After the planes were parked and chocks placed on either side of the tires, the rear cargo door was lowered, and the three GAZ 23304 Tigers rolled down the ramp first, followed by the snowplow. Four soldiers got into each of the Tigers and two into the snowplow, with the remaining unit members staying with the aircraft.

With the snowplow leading the way, the military convoy worked its way through the two inches of snow which covered the local streets, the depth of snow increasing to four inches as they left the town and pulled onto the Kolyma Highway, where plowing was less frequent. Because road conditions required them to drive more cautiously, and the unfamiliar highway lacked lighting, it took seven hours to reach Myaundzha. The four vehicles pulled into the café at six-thirty in the morning to refuel and get a bite to eat, parking beside a snowplow with an extension cord running from its block heater to an outlet atop a metal pole.

Although the four military vehicles also had block heaters, they were designed to be connected to generators. Therefore, their extension cords were only ten feet in length. The problem that Durchenko faced was that there was only one outside outlet, and the civilian snowplow was connected to it. He could disconnect and use the outlet without consequence. However, a check of the vehicle revealed the keys weren't inside, so he'd need to find the owner to move it. However, one outlet would not satisfy his needs. His military vehicles were dependable in the extreme cold once they started, but it was the toss of a coin whether the engines would turn over in minus fifty degrees plus weather without the block heater connected. As a result, he ordered that they be left running.

When the lieutenant colonel and his men walked into the small café, the door triggered a chime, and the owner entered the room a minute later to find fourteen men seated at the four Formica-topped tables.

"Where can I fuel my vehicles?" the lieutenant colonel asked, summoning the owner to him with a wave of his hand.

The owner pointed to the side of the house, saying he had a heated and vented underground fuel tank ten feet below the surface, keeping the fuel in a narrow range of temperatures. Therefore, refueling his military vehicles wouldn't be an issue even in this extreme cold.

""Where are the menus?" Durchenko asked, receiving a response that the café only served two dishes, Stroganina and Indigirka salad, and one dessert, Kyorchekh.

Despite the groans from his men, who would have preferred a carnivorous meal over plates of fish, the lieutenant colonel ordered the entire menu for each man, after which the owner left for his kitchen.

Because the food was served cold, the twenty-eight plates of Stroganina and Indigirka salad were on the tables within twenty minutes, and the soldiers quickly consumed their food.

"Do you operate the snowplow outside?" Durchenko asked the owner, who cleared the dishes before bringing out dessert.

"One of the town's residents has a contract with the government to clear a long stretch of highway on either side of the town."

"This storm must have kept him busy."

"He's always busy during the winter and well-paid for his work. If he doesn't keep his section clear, a dozen residents will report him to the transportation office in Yakutsk and volunteer to replace him since his snowplow belongs to the government. That's why I was surprised he took those foreigners to Ust Nera and ignored the roads for half a day."

"What?" Durchenko said in surprise. "These foreigners?" he asked, removing a packet of photos from his jacket pocket and handing them to him.

"Yes."

"How do you know he drove them to Ust Nera?"

"There are only two directions you can go on the Kolyma Highway. If you turn left at the end of my drive, the next population center is Ust Nera. If you turn right, you'll go to Tomtor and Oymyakon. He turned left. Since he was gone for half a day, I guessed he went to Ust Nera."

"He could have plowed for that long."

"He would need to come here and refuel. That he didn't means he refueled someplace else, and Ust Nera and Tomtor are the nearest refueling stations."

Durchenko remained silent for the next fifteen seconds, stroking his neck as he thought.

"Four people plus the driver couldn't fit in the cab of that snowplow, and no one could be in the truck bed for that long because they'd freeze to death before reaching Ust Nera."

"As you can see, the area outside my café is always well-lit at night to attract customers. That's how I saw the two women getting into the cab with the driver while the two men climbed into the truck's bed. The driver handed the men propane heaters and fur pelts. They'd be warm enough to survive for five hours."

"Where does this snowplow driver live?"

The owner told him.

"This is for the food and fuel we'll pump," Durchenko said, putting a stack of rubles on the table. "Don't tell anyone about our conversation."

The eight-hour flight from Omsk to Moscow seemed to drag on forever, the en-route refueling providing some relief from the cramped interior of the Cessna and everyone's impatience to get to Moscow. An hour from landing, the pilot asked Olena, sitting in the co-pilot's seat, where she wanted to land, the only caveat being that it had to be on snow for obvious reasons. She asked Wayan.

Because he didn't know the first thing about Moscow, Wayan wanted to call Tjay and ask where they should land. However, he didn't want to give the FSB that location in case they were listening. Therefore, he told Olena to ask the pilot, who he was sure knew a strip of snow in Moscow where they could land and not attract attention, what he would suggest.

"The Myachkovo Airport," Belevich responded. "It has ten times more skiplanes flights than Omsk, and it's far from Moscow's four major airports. That means we can land without worrying that a low-flying plane will run over us. Also, the bush pilots mind their own business and expect the same from others. Therefore, if the FSB later comes and asks them questions, everyone will have amnesia whether they saw you."

"Which makes that airport the perfect choice. How far is it from the city?" Persik asked.

"It's nineteen miles southeast."

The skiplane landed at eleven-thirty in the evening, smoothly setting down on the patch of snow the airport maintained for bush pilots. It was parallel to the row of open hangars used by them, an open hangar meaning there were no doors and that both ends were open to the outside.

As the aircraft taxied to a hangar, Wayan called Tjay and told them they'd landed at Myachkovo.

"I know the airport. Go to the executive terminal and wait. Someone will be there in approximately thirty minutes."

Olena was the last of the fugitives to get off the plane. As the pilot began closing the aircraft's door, she asked if he was returning to Omsk.

"I don't know where my next flight will be," he replied. "Someone will come to the hangar or call and tell me what they want transported and where it's to be delivered. Once we agree on a price, I go. It's the same for all skiplane pilots. Depending on how many planes are waiting, I could be here for an hour or a day or more."

"And if we're again in need of your services?"

He wrote a phone number on a piece of paper that he ripped from his notepad. "Call this number."

At seven in the morning, Durchenko and his men burst into the truck driver's home and dragged him out of bed while the others searched the five hundred square feet house. It didn't take long to find the stacks of rubles given to him by Wayan, stuffed inside a satchel in the closet. When shown the money, the truck driver started to say something, but Durchenko told him to shut up. The driver obeyed, shaking in fear beside the bed in his dirty thermal underwear.

"You will not tell me a lie or half-truth," the lieutenant colonel stated. "Instead, you'll give me the details of what you did to get this money, starting with how you first met the four fugitives. If you tell the truth, I won't torture you to extract the information. If you lie, you're going to wish you were dead. Is that clear?"

The driver nodded and, without further prompting, gave the officer a rendition of events from the time he encountered the bus stuck in the snow until the four fugitives chartered a Yakutia Airlines plane to take them to Moscow.

"They never boarded the train," the lieutenant colonel said. That was clever. What time was this?"

"Around four, yesterday afternoon."

"And you're sure of the airline?"

"Yakutia is the only airline in Ust Nera."

"Who did they speak with at the airline?"

"They told me the manager arranged for the flight."

"Is there anything else you can remember?"

The driver said there wasn't.

Durchenko walked away and phoned Lazarev's aide. It was midnight in Moscow, but the aide was awake, trying to chip away at the pile of papers on his desk. On receiving the lieutenant colonel's call and, knowing the general wouldn't want to hear a secondhand summation of what he said, he conferenced him into the conversation. Durchenko then told them what he'd learned.

"There's an FSB team in Ust Nera. I'll take it from here," the general stated. "You and your unit can return to Novosibirsk."

Durchenko wanted to say that he had men at the airport, and they were as good if not better than the FSB team and capable of apprehending and questioning the airline manager. He understood why the general wanted to send the military down a treacherous Siberian highway in extreme weather instead of assigning the mission to the FSB, knowing the military had the necessary equipment and could deploy it rapidly. However, it irked him that, because of Lazarev, the FSB team had the hometown advantage and that his unit had no further role to play. But, not wanting to risk his career, he kept his opinions to himself and acknowledged his orders.

Once Durchenko finished his call, he told his men they were going back to the café to refuel and returning to Ust Nera.

"What about him?" one of Durchenko's men asked, pointing to the driver.

Durchenko, holding the satchel in his left hand, pulled his handgun with his right and put a round into the center of the driver's forehead.

"Problem solved," he said.

Nazarov and two of his men arrived at the manager's house at the edge of town thirty minutes after receiving Lazarev's call. The manager, who knew that no story would be good enough to obfuscate the truth, told him everything and showed him her hiding place under a loose floorboard in her kitchen, where she hid the rubles.

"How long does it take to fly to Moscow?"

"In the AN-140, ten hours, which includes an hour to refuel along the way, because the turboprop doesn't have the range to fly there nonstop."

"They're already in Moscow," he irritably stated. "Can you tell me where they landed?"

"Only if I access my airport computer. I don't have remote access."

"Let's go."

Tjay knew that, although the FSB hadn't historically committed their resources to following embassy staff, that would change following Olena's abduction by three Indonesians. He also knew that the decryption of their embassy's conversations would become a priority. Therefore, he didn't have much time to retrieve the four fugitives from the airport before the FSB would be there in force. Because the embassy had a staff of forty, the FSB couldn't follow everyone and would focus on senior officials. As a result, he tasked the most junior consulate with leaving early, renting a large SUV, and getting the four fugitives. He'd then take them to the safehouse, a dacha twenty-five miles from the city and forty miles from the Myachkovo Airport.

A dacha is a cottage-like home that's usually in a tiny village or colony outside a population center. The Russians view it as a place to temporarily escape the grind of urban life, reconnect with nature, and enjoy time with family and friends. Sixty million Russians own Dachas within the country, most of which sit vacant during the winter.

The dacha to which the four fugitives were taken was a pale green single-story wooden structure bordered by a picket fence that had seen better days. The three-bedroom structure looked no different than any other on the road, all of which were constructed between 1950 and 1960. However, unlike the other dachas, this one was primarily used in the winter when the others were vacant, guaranteeing the privacy of those staying there.

Although the road going past the dacha was unplowed, the GMC Yukon had no problem getting to it, and the four went inside after the junior consulate pressed the code on the keyless door lock. Because the dacha was winterized and everything except the electricity shut off, the inside was only heated to forty degrees Fahrenheit, which was warm enough to keep things from freezing and, although still cold, twenty-five degrees warmer than outside.

Once inside, the junior consulate cranked up the heat to seventy-four, built a fire to speed up getting warm, and turned on the water heater so everyone could take a hot shower. When the chill subsided, he put out the packets of meat and cheese that Tjay gave him before leaving the embassy, knowing the four fugitives would be hungry.

"Is tomorrow the day you're freeing my husband?" Olena asked him as the other fugitives began to eat.

The junior associate responded he didn't know.

"When can we speak with Tjay?" Wayan asked.

The junior associate again responded he didn't know.

"What do you know?" Persik asked in frustration.

"If anything happens to Olena Kuzma, I'll be transferred to our consulate in Pyongyang, North Korea."

"The plane never made it to Moscow. It's at the Tsentralny Omsk Airport," the manager told Nazarov as she looked at the display on her Yakutia Airlines computer screen.

"You told me they were going to Moscow, not Omsk."

"The aircraft refueled there but, according to the pilot's notes, couldn't leave because the airport closed due to bad weather."

"That means they're still in Omsk."

The manager, not knowing where the four passengers were, didn't comment.

"I want to speak with the pilot. Give me his number," Nazarov demanded.

She got his cellphone number from the computer and gave it to him.

After saving the number on his cellphone, Nazarov put his hand on the grip of his gun, believing he should kill the woman because she was of no further use and knew too much. However, thinking better of it, he decided that killing her was premature since he hadn't spoken to the Yakutia aircrew and didn't know the location of the fugitives. He moved his hand from the grip.

"Keep her under guard, and don't let her leave the terminal," Nazarov said.

The manager, who thought she was going to die, fainted.

The captain of the chartered Yakutia Airlines turboprop was asleep in the Aero Hotel, a one-minute walk from the VIP lounge, when he was awoken at five in the morning by a call from someone with an unlisted number. Irritated, he turned off his phone and went back to sleep, believing it was another unsolicited caller trying to sell him something he didn't need. Fifty minutes later, two airport security guards entered his room and woke him up, Nazarov having an FSB tech get the captain's GPS coordinates from his phone.

"Turn on your phone," one guard said.

The captain did.

It took less than five minutes for Nazarov to determine that the pilot did not know where his passengers had gone, only glimpsing them in the VIP lounge before going to the hotel. His next call to the VIP lounge didn't go any better, learning the hostess on duty wasn't there when the four fugitives entered the lounge. However, she gave him the number of the hostess on duty the previous evening, who told him they took a shuttle to the skiplane hangar.

"Why go there if the airport was closed?" Nazarov asked.

"They're private pilots not filing a flight plan. They're not subject to the same rules as commercial airlines and can come and go as they please, even in the worst conditions."

"I need to speak to the person in charge of that facility."

"No one is in charge. It's an open hangar where skiplane's enter and leave day and night. They don't use the airport's runway; they use a runway of snow adjacent to the hangar to takeoff and land."

Nazarov sent the airport security guards to the hangar to see if anyone saw the four fugitives, whose descriptions he gave to the guards. Abuzz with activity, just as the hostess said, none of the bush pilots had been there for longer than ninety minutes.

When the call ended, the colonel slammed his fist onto the airline counter in frustration. The four fugitives were still in the wind.

8

It was four in the morning when Nazarov woke up Lazarev's aide and said that the fugitives hired a skiplane to fly them out of Omsk. The aide, who'd been asleep for two hours, asked him to repeat what he'd said to ensure he got it right and, understanding the seriousness of what he heard, conferenced in the general. That conversation took place three hours after the fugitives arrived at the dacha.

"When did they leave Omsk?" the general asked.

Nazarov gave his best estimate.

"Assume they're here. Using a skiplane, they could land on a patch of snow a quarter mile long."

Nazarov, the messenger of the bad news, remained silent.

Lazarev told his aide to check with military and airport radar systems to see if they'd tracked a low-flying plane landing in an area other than an airport in the last twelve hours.

The colonel cleared his throat and said that he'd already checked and was told the radar surrounding Moscow couldn't function below two hundred feet because of ground clutter.

"If they're in Moscow, they would have communicated with someone to pick them up. I'll check with the SSCI," the aide volunteered, referring to the FSBs Service of Special Communications and Information function.

"Have them look at calls to the Indonesian embassy's senior staff and put each of them under surveillance," the general added. "And colonel, don't return to Yakutsk yet. Take a military aircraft to Moscow. You seem to know what's happening with these fugitives better than anyone, and your insights could be invaluable. Bring your team. They may also be useful."

Fedir Kuzma learned of his accelerated relocation to Kubinka Airbase when Colonel Aleksei Assonov barged into his lab at nine in the morning and told him of the move.

"I thought that was in four days," Kuzma shot back.

"The schedule has changed. Start packing your work papers and computer. The lab assistants and my men will box your equipment," he said, pointing to the heavy cardboard boxes and packing material they were bringing into the lab. "I want to be out of here by eleven."

Kuzma was in a panic. Tjay had given him the time and method for his extraction and transport to the safehouse, which wouldn't work if he were moved to the base because he didn't believe they'd let him come nineteen miles for a daily cup of coffee. Another problem was informing Tjay because Assonov wanted to be gone by eleven, an hour before they usually met. He needed to find a way to stay in Moscow until the extraction time, or his Indonesian contact found an alternative way to rescue him.

So far, he'd held back the technologically innovative part of his work so that, when he left, the Russians only had the hardware configuration they would have eventually figured out. However, the software that made his design work was an entirely different matter and out of his control.

"Now, doctor," Assonov commanded, seeing that he hadn't moved.

Kuzma grabbed his leather briefcase off the floor. He wasn't a medical doctor, but he was smart enough to know that only a medical emergency requiring immediate care would keep him from going to the base. He could fake a heart attack by collapsing and saying his chest felt like an elephant was sitting on it, but that wouldn't get him much of a delay. As soon as they took his vitals at the hospital and the doctor saw that his blood didn't have a raised troponin level, the protein an indicator of a heart attack, he'd be on his way to Kubinka. Therefore, he needed to create an actual medical emergency that brought him to the brink of death. However, he didn't have time to search the internet on how to do this.

As he complied with Assonov's order to pack, thinking about how to create a medical emergency as he did, he opened the top drawer of his desk and began putting its contents into his briefcase. Seeing his blood pressure medicine gave him an idea.

The blood pressure medicine he was taking was a beta blocker, which worked by inhibiting the effects of the hormone epinephrine, or adrenalin, causing a slower heartbeat. Seeing no other option, he popped four pills and shoved the bottle to the back of the drawer where it'd be difficult to see. Acting normally, he began placing papers into his briefcase. He felt fine and wondered if he'd taken enough pills or if the effect would occur once he left the lab or was at the airbase. That concern left his mind when, fifteen minutes later, he became lightheaded and short of breath. Disoriented and staggering, he grabbed for the counter to steady himself, missed, and collapsed onto the floor.

Assonov was standing less than ten feet from Kuzma when he saw him fall. The look of confusion on the doctor's face and how he fell showed he wasn't faking. After telling one of his men to call for an ambulance, he knelt beside him, determined he was breathing, and put two fingers to his carotid artery to feel for a pulse. It was barely detectable. Unable to do anything more before the medics arrived, he called Lazarev's aide and told him what had happened. The aide immediately forwarded the call to Lazarev.

"Are you certain he's not faking it?" the general asked, suspicious of the timing of Kuzma's purported illness after being told what occurred and that an ambulance was on its way.

"It looks like a heart attack. He couldn't fake the low pulse, shallow breathing, and dilated pupils," was the reply. "His skin is also clammy and white."

"The stress may have been too much for him. Seal the lab and place a guard outside so no one gets in without my approval. When the ambulance arrives, stay beside him on the way to the hospital, and ensure his room is heavily guarded and that he's accompanied if he leaves it for a test."

While waiting for the ambulance, the colonel went to the most senior of Kuzma's four lab assistants, all of whom were assigned by the Russian Academy of Sciences and considered experts in camouflage technology. While their job was to assist the doctor, their focus was to learn everything they could about his research so they could duplicate his work if necessary and continue it at the Ministry of Science.

"Can you continue his work if he dies?" Assonov asked.

"While the hardware systems he's designed are creative and complex in attempting to make something visually transparent when in motion, we're only six months to a year away in duplicating these innovations."

"You're saying that his death will have a minimal impact," Assonov stated.

"If we're talking about the hardware, which I liken to the body. The software is the brain. We're years behind in developing software that effectively tells the body what to do. In other words, how to operate the multi-faceted camouflage technology when something is in motion."

"Why wasn't I told about the software?" the colonel angrily asked.

"In complex systems, computer programming is done at the end so that the programs don't have to be continually changed as the hardware is perfected. Even a small modification can cause significant changes in the software. If we make software changes as the hardware develops, glitches are common because of conflicting instructions and patches. These additional lines of code also slow computations. In a phrase, changing the software as you go slows program development. As to why you didn't know, I was told you were here for security."

The colonel controlled his temper not to bite the head of this arrogant prick. "What you're telling me is that if he dies, his hardware is a pile of useless scrap, no better than our pile of useless crap because neither has a brain."

"You're entirely correct. He's a genius at hardware design, but that pales compared to the intellect required to write the software for such a complex system. At the Academy, we have a building filled with engineers working day and night trying to write and perfect such software. Therefore, I don't know how Doctor Kuzma could have the time to perfect his hardware and work on the software."

"What are you implying?" Assonov asked, giving the tech a puzzled look.

"If you see a software engineer, their hands fly on their keyboard, and they exude confidence. I don't see that when Dr. Kuzma is on his computer, which leads me to suspect that someone else is writing the software."

"When were you planning to tell me your suspicions?"

"Again, I view you as security. I was planning to tell the Academy after an upcoming test of the hardware where a software update was required."

Assonov thought back to his briefings prior to kidnapping Kuzma and his wife. Not once was it mentioned that hardware and software developments were on separate tracks, although it now seemed that should have been obvious. Someone, or a group of someones, assumed that Doctor Fedir Kuzma did both. They were wrong.

"Could they hire a person to write the operating system after the hardware design is complete?"

"Not usually. They're customarily hired at the beginning because an intimate understanding of how the system works is necessary to write the complicated instructions to operate the hardware. If Kuzma dies, I have no idea how we'll find that person."

"I do," Assonov said.

Kevin Tjay was running on fumes. After dispatching the junior consulate to pick up the four fugitives nine hours ago, he grabbed a few hours of sleep on the couch in his office before continuing to try and figure out how to get the Kuzma's out of Russia. If he couldn't, he'd be forced to ask the Americans or one of his country's other allies for help and risk handing them the scientist's advanced technology and getting little, if anything, in return.

Looking out the window of his office with the binoculars he kept on his desk, he saw the usual FSB van parked across from the embassy, along with a similar unmarked van at either end of the street. To him, this sudden ratcheting of surveillance was a clear sign the FSB believed the embassy was involved in Olena Kuzma's escape. It was also a safe bet to conclude that he and other embassy staff members would be closely watched on leaving the building.

Moscow traffic was in full force on the narrow street below when he heard a siren and saw an ambulance slowly weaving between vehicles before parking in front of the government building across the street and wheeling a gurney inside. Putting down the binoculars and taking a camera with a telephoto lens from his bottom desk drawer, he waited to photograph whoever the medics would wheel out of the building, hoping it might prove helpful to the Badan Intelijen Negara, or BIN, the country's premier intelligence agency.

After a fifteen-minute wait, they pushed the gurney outside. His eyes widened in surprise, and his mouth went agape as he zoomed in on Fedir Kuzma's face. As his heart rate accelerated rapidly, he snapped photo after photo of the scientist and those beside the gurney, one of them a thick-chested colonel wearing the Russian Army uniform.

Realizing that something serious had happened to the defector, he considered two possibilities, both of which were bad. The first was that if the scientist died, he still needed to get Olena Kuzma and the three non-tourists clandestinely out of the country because, if caught, they'd expose his government illegally operating on Russian soil. That task became nearly impossible with Kuzma's death because no country would risk their sources and methods for extracting the four fugitives without receiving something significant in return. Therefore, living in denial, he assumed the scientist survived without suffering a stroke or similar impairment and there was another shot at a rescue.

Beginning to look at the situation calmly and unemotionally, which was difficult considering what he saw, he realized that the first step in finding out the scientist's health was to know where the ambulance was taking him. The most obvious way of doing this was to follow it. However, with the enhanced embassy surveillance, he'd have an escort that may or may not let him follow the ambulance despite his diplomatic plates. Therefore, he needed another way to determine where it was going.

A few taps on his keyboard showed there were thirty-three medical centers in Moscow. Tjay had only been to one, the Russian Academy of Sciences Hospital in a wooded area nine miles west of the Kremlin, when he visited the ambassador following an emergency appendectomy. The ambassador told him that he believed they took him there because senior Kremlin officials considered it the best hospital in Russia, and the government didn't want to be accused of having subpar medical care if anything happened to a foreign dignitary. Considering Kuzma's importance and the trouble the government went through to kidnap him in Ukraine, he believed the doctor was destined for the same hospital. However, he knew that was a guess coupled with wishful thinking.

However, regardless of the hospital, the question was how to determine his medical condition because Russian hospitals were notorious for being tight-lipped about a patient's condition, especially those guarded by the FSB. If he scaled that mountain and discovered Kuzma was ambulatory, he needed to find a way to separate him from his security detail and get him out of the hospital and to the safehouse without being followed.

Time also worked against him because, if Kuzma was alive and ambulatory, they might take him to the airbase without returning to his lab across the street. For all he knew, that could be later today. Therefore, he needed to act quickly.

The ability to rescue the doctor in his current situation was beyond the capabilities of Wayan and his team, requiring local knowledge and resources. With time rapidly working against him, Tjay went to the ambassador's office and asked permission to call a person whose number his predecessor had given them, and whose services the embassy used when there was no other option. The caveat the official he replaced told him was that, although this person had a reputation for getting anything done within the Russian Federation, he was not to be trusted. Asked to explain, his predecessor said: "He's a mercenary who shops the deal."

"Meaning?"

"Soliciting someone he knows wants you hurt, dead, or kidnapped and offering to do it for a price."

"After the contract?" Tjay asked his predecessor.

"He always fulfills his contracts."

There are over five thousand organized crime groups in Russia. The largest, with annual revenues of eight and a half billion dollars, is the Solntsevskaya Bratva, or Bratva, as most refer to it. Its leader, Sergei Burkov, is five feet seven inches in height and built like a fire hydrant, meaning he had a stocky build, thick arms and legs, and an almost unnoticeable neck. His eyes were coal black, cynical, and gave the simultaneous impression of contempt and shrewdness. The fifty-six-year-old had short black hair and a deep, resonant voice.

Burkov was a savvy businessperson, performing off-the-books services for senior government officials, oligarchs, heads of corporations, and others of influence because of his reputation for always fulfilling his contract. When he agreed to make something happen, it did. His only requirement was that whatever he was asked to do be within the borders of the Russian Federation. Outside that demarcation line, he left the illegal activities in which he specialized to other organized crime groups. The reason for this geographical limitation was that he didn't want foreign law enforcement organizations demanding the Russian government reign in the Bratva's illicit foreign activities. That scrutiny was bad for business. Therefore, by restricting the Bratva's operation to the Russian Federation, coupled with those in influential positions protecting him for both the services he provided and what he knew, and those in law enforcement and the judiciary, government officials, business owners, and hundreds more he bribed to look the other way, the Bratva operated within the country as if it was another branch of government.

Tjay knew that, although Burkov couldn't get the Kuzma's out of the country because the Bratva operated exclusively within its confines, he could get Fedir Kuzma out of the hospital and to the safehouse—if he was alive. He thought about hiring him to rescue Olena Kuzma from Oymyakon and her husband from the lab instead of using the three non-tourists. However, aware of his predecessor's warning, he determined the downside could be substantial. In figuring out what that might be, he believed once the Bratva leader fulfilled his contract and, knowing Fedir

Kuzma's importance and how much the Russian government wanted him, he'd find a way to profit off that knowledge and make his abduction up to the government by selling the location of the safehouse. That was a win-win for the organized crime leader because he would have fulfilled his contract while giving the government what it wanted: Fadir and Olena Kuzma. However, with his back to the wall, he had no choice but to use Burkov and afterward find a way to get the Kuzma's out of the country as quickly as possible.

Once the ambassador approved hiring the crime leader, Tjay called and requested an immediate meeting. The Bratva leader only negotiated a contract face-to-face because the government monitored and recorded all domestic voice and data communications, and he didn't want to tip his hand. Burkov didn't go to these meetings. Instead, he sent one of his lieutenants with authority to negotiate a deal.

They sealed the contract after a thirty-minute meeting and confirmation that the money was received in an offshore account. Burkov's lieutenant said that assuming Fedir Kuzma was alive, the extraction would occur soon.

"It needs to happen before he's taken to the airbase," Tjay said.

"This extraction takes preparation, but it's possible that it could happen as soon as today."

"And if he's taken to the airbase?"

"Extraction is still possible but very costly."

"How costly?" Tjay asked, knowing the current fee wasn't cheap.

"Ten times what you're paying."

Tjay didn't respond, knowing his contingency fund wasn't bottomless and, given what Wayan had spent and what Burkov's lieutenant was asking, it was near depletion.

The crime boss's lieutenant, seeing that the official was stunned at the amount he'd be asking, explained it was costly because he'd need to bribe senior officials in both the FSB and the Air Force who'd face a lifetime in prison or death if the government discovered their role in Kuzma's escape. "Where do you want the doctor delivered?" the lieutenant asked, returning to why he was there.

Tjay wrote the address of the dacha and handed him the slip of paper.

9

The FSBs Service of Special Communications and Information was responsible for the real-time decryption of communications and data traffic within the homeland. Because some encryptions are more complex, the time to decrypt them varies widely. The communications between Tjay and Wayan were complicated because the Indonesian government used an encryption key developed by the US government. Although it was two generations removed from the latest NSA system, it required numerous hours of brute-force computations by FSB supercomputers to break, the result being that at five that evening, sixteen hours after the fugitives arrived at the dacha and eight after Fedir Kuzma was taken to the hospital, Lazarev had a copy of Tjay and Wayan's conversations. He summoned Nazarov to his office, the colonel arriving thirty minutes later and was shown the conversations.

"Our fugitives have been getting help from the Deputy Chief of Mission at the Indonesian embassy. The money he wired allowed them to get to the Myachkovo Airport, where they were picked up and taken to a safehouse," Nazarov summarized.

"The security camera at the VIP terminal identified the vehicle as a GMC Yukon, rented by a junior consulate at the embassy," Lazarev continued, providing photos of the vehicle that showed the four fugitives leaving the terminal and getting into it.

"Where did they go?" Nazarov asked, wanting to cut to the chase.

"Because most Moscow rental car agencies install GPS trackers to locate the vehicles in case of theft, we found the rental a dacha forty miles from the airport. Here's a photo," he said, handing Nazarov the eight-by-ten print of the dacha. "I ordered the surveillance team not to park in clusters and pull into empty dachas' driveways at least two miles away. The last thing we want is to be seen before your team arrives.

"You want my men to do the takedown rather than agents from Lubyanka?" Nazarov asked, wondering if he heard the general correctly.

"Using agents from a distant field office has the advantage of secrecy and privacy," Lazarev responded. "Sometimes, size works against you when containing information."

Nazarov wasn't buying it. If there was anything the FSB prided itself on was its historical and current ability to keep a secret. He knew firsthand that they ingrained it in the psyche and habits of every employee, no matter the position. The better explanation was that if things went sideways and the fugitives escaped or caused negative publicity, he'd take the fall for Lazarev. In the west, what the general was doing was called CYA, standing for cover your ass.

"Understood," Nazarov replied.

Tjay saw four men strolling on the sidewalk outside the embassy, reappearing twenty minutes later going in the same direction. It was cold outside, even for a Muscovite. Although he believed one person might be crazy enough to stroll around the block in this weather, he didn't think four shared that insanity. The more logical conclusion was that they were there to prevent the fugitives from entering the embassy, where they'd be untouchable.

As he looked out the window, the ambassador called and said he was leaving the embassy, having been summoned to the Minister of Foreign Affairs office. With everything else that happened, it confirmed the FSB had broken the embassy's encryption keys, and it was only a matter of time until they had the address of the dacha. The timing couldn't have been worse. If Burkov's men delivered Kuzma this evening, the FSB would have everyone they were after in one place.

Tjay phoned the junior consulate. "The dacha has been compromised. Get everyone out of there as quickly as possible before the FSB arrives."

"Where do we go?"

"Find a place. Get out of there now."

"What about the last person in our group?" the junior consulate hurriedly asked, referring to Fedir Kuzma.

"I'll have the delivery service hold him until I figure out how to get him to you. Go."

Tjay's next call was to Burkov's lieutenant, telling him that if the package was going to be delivered tonight, he needed to hold onto it longer because he wasn't sure of the delivery location."

"We're not babysitters," was the response.

"Babysitters get a twenty percent bonus."

"Twenty-five."

"Deal."

He was about to say something else when his phone died. The internet was also down. Similar complaints soon cropped up from other embassy employees. The Russians had jammed every electronic signal into and out of the embassy.

The four fugitives and the junior consulate left the dacha within two minutes of Tjay's call. Although it was snowing heavily, the GMC Yukon held the road like a summer day as they distanced themselves from the dacha.

"Did Tjay say how the FSB discovered the dacha?" Wayan asked the junior consulate.

"He didn't, but I assume they broke our encryption."

"That's a plausible explanation."

"Is there another?"

"Is this Yukon a rental, or does it belong to an individual because it doesn't have diplomatic plates?"

"It's a rental."

"Most rental cars have GPS trackers so the company can locate the vehicle if it's stolen. It's not inconceivable that's how they discovered us. Let's make sure. Stop the car," Wayan said.

The junior associate did, and Wayan crawled under the vehicle, returning five minutes later holding a battery. When he got back inside, he tossed it to Persik.

"A GPS tracking device," Persik stated, having placed them on the cars of bad guys, as did Wayan when he was a detective. "If anyone were tracking us, this would be our last known position," he said, rolling down the window and tossing the battery outside.

As Wayan was disabling the GPS tracker, Nazarov and his men, having been given tactical gear and equipment, battered down the front door of the Indonesian dacha. As he entered the kitchen, the colonel's eyes focused on the counter where a swish had been drawn on a piece of paper, the same work of art Olena Kuzma had left for her FSB guard in Oymyakon. Uttering a string of profanities, he removed his handgun from its holster and emptied half the clip into the swish, shredding it. Hearing gunfire, his men rushed into the kitchen, lowering their weapons when they saw the colonel's target.

"The garage is empty," one of his men said as the colonel holstered his gun.

Without responding, Nazarov went outside into the frigid air to collect his thoughts. He realized he'd screwed up in not verifying the Yukon was at the dacha before his assaut. Removing the phone from his pocket, he called the tech who'd given Lazarev the tracking data and asked for the vehicle's location.

"The signal went dead twenty minutes ago," the tech answered.

"Meaning they're in a dead spot?"

"The tracker interacts with a satellite. There are no dead spots. The lack of a signal means the device either malfunctioned or, more likely, has been disabled."

Nazarov stood motionless as he tried to understand how three Indonesians and the doctor's wife, who he believed was the software genius enabling her husband's hardware, eluded the world's most sophisticated domestic security apparatus. Believing they were smart enough to understand they couldn't elude capture within the Russian Federation forever, he thought their gathering at the dacha was a prelude to leaving the country and that somehow Fedir Kuzma would accompany them. He didn't know how they would accomplish that, given the tight security he was under at the hospital, but he wasn't going to discount their creativity because, so far, they were kicking his ass.

The Russian Academy of Sciences, established by Peter the Great in 1724, is a network of scientific research institutes, libraries, publishing units, and hospitals. Fedir Kuzma's room was on the fifth floor of the four-hundred-bed Moscow facility, which had the latest medical and clinical equipment from manufacturers across the globe because it served the Kremin. As the elite was constantly visiting the facility, security was tight. Army guards patrolled he walled academy compound, with two-person teams stationed at each entrance.

The emergency entrance for walk-ins and those arriving by ambulance was on the west side. Burkov's men had entered through that portal in the past, but never to get a patient. Instead, hired by a senior Kremlin official who wanted to eliminate a rival and make their death appear to result from their medical condition, they went inside to kill someone. Therefore, although familiar with how to get into and out of the facility without attracting attention, bringing out a patient who, if alive, was assumed to be non-ambulatory required more creativity. In the end, it was Burkov who came up with the solution for that.

The rescue began at five-thirty in the afternoon Moscow time, ten minutes before Nazarov and his men burst into the Indonesian embassy's dacha, when an ambulance from a well-known provider arrived at the emergency entrance. Two of Burkov's men, dressed as emergency medical technicians and wearing the replicated ID badges of the provider, unloaded the gurney on which another Bratva soldier was laying. A large white sheet covered the pseudo-patient, underneath which he wore scrubs and a replicated hospital ID.

As in their previous visits, the pseudo-patient was wheeled past the guards at the emergency entrance and into the hospital. Once inside, the cart was pushed into a recessed area, and he hopped off.

"Five minutes," one guard said to the pseudo-patient, who confirmed that timing with a nod.

Once the two soldiers left, the pseudo-patient straightened the white sheet on the gurney and rolled it into the elevator, pressing the button for the fifth floor. When the doors opened, he pushed the gurney down the hall, stopping at a room with two plainclothes guards beside the door.

"I'm here to take Dr. Kuzma to radiology," the pseudo-patient said.

One guard looked closely at his ID card, which showed he worked in that department.

"No one informed us," the other guard responded as he and his partner moved in front of the door to block entry into the room.

"The scan will take fifteen minutes. You're welcome to stay with me the entire time."

The guards talked it over, concluding that interfering with Kuzma's medical care wasn't a good career move and, since he was sedated and had an IV line in his arm, he wasn't going to escape.

Coupled with the offer to accompany the tech and stay with him, they allowed him to leave the room.

The hospital's Department of Radiology was large and constantly busy, its thirty-five diagnostic and treatment rooms comprising the ground floor of the east wing. The department employed two hundred-fifty technicians, doctors, and administrative staff, each working twelve hours shifts, four days per week. Therefore, in contrast to the fifth floor, which was quiet and had a small nursing staff, radiology was organized chaos, with patients constantly coming and going. If someone had a hospital ID card, their presence went unchallenged.

"You'll need to turn off your cell phones if you want to come inside," the pseudo-patient said, pointing to a large sign on the door. "Cellular frequencies interfere with the diagnostic equipment."

The guards, seeing the sign, complied.

The pseudo-patient's phone vibrated, and he read a message on his screen. Pretending to turn off his phone, he briskly wheeled the gurney down the hall until he found the room number that appeared on his screen and wheeled Kuzma inside.

"We need to wait in the hall until the tech finishes the magnetic scan. We can't be in the room during the test because of the metal on us."

The guards were uneasy having Kuzma out of their sight. However, because the person who'd taken him to radiology would wait with them, and they knew that some radiology machines generated a strong magnetic field and neither wanted to strip and wear a hospital gown to comply, they accepted the tech's explanation and followed him out of the room.

"You said this would take fifteen minutes," one guard reminded him.

"It Takes a few minutes to prep the patient and twelve for the procedure. Fifteen minutes," the pseudo-patient reiterated.

One feature of the radiology department was that every diagnostic and treatment room had a front and rear entrance. The back entrance was off a hallway that ran parallel to the patient corridor and was used by doctors and techs to enter and leave the room. To the side of that corridor were a cluster of doctor's offices, nurses' cubicles, and medical supply stations. This design meant the patients would transit a single corridor— whether walking, in a wheelchair, or on a gurney. The parallel hallway was designed to be used by staff to avoid the congestion of a singular hallway. Once Kuzma was alone in the room, the pseudo-patient said he needed a bathroom break. Both guards agreed it was better to remain outside the radiology room than accompany him. Therefore, they watched as the tech walked down the patient corridor in the opposite direction from where they'd come and turned into a side hallway.

As soon as the pseudo-patient turned into the side hallway, he ran to the parallel connecting corridor, turned left, and rushed to the rear hospital exit. Because the door could only be opened from the inside, no army guards were posted outside. He stepped into the rear of the ambulance, closing the doors as it sped away.

When the pseudo-patient didn't return in ten minutes, the guards realized something was wrong and, procedure or not, entered the radiology room. Seeing the gurney was gone and the room had a back door, they threw it open and streaked down the parallel corridor and out the rear exit. However, by that time, the three Bratva soldiers had already discarded the ambulance and moved Kuzma to a minivan.

Following Wayan's disabling of the GPS tracker, the junior associate spent the next twenty minutes distancing himself from their last know position, stopping when he saw a dacha one hundred yards off the road with no neighbor in sight.

"What do you think?" he asked Wayan.

"We've driven far enough and should see if anyone is home."

The junior consulate pulled onto the gravel path and parked in front of the garage. Wayan, the first out of the vehicle, took a tire iron from the cargo compartment and went to the front door.

"What's that for?" Persik asked, looking at what he was carrying.

"It's my key to the dacha."

After pounding on the door and not receiving a response, Wayan used it to break the lock. He used the same key to open the garage so the vehicle could pull inside.

A quick check revealed that the electricity and water had been turned off. Therefore, the interior of the dacha was nearly as cold as the outside.

"Let's take a few of those logs and throw them in the fireplace. I'm freezing," Persik said, pointing to the stack.

"The smoke will be seen for miles," Wayan replied.

"Then let's go back to the car and turn on the heater," Persik said, his teeth chattering.

"We'd need to leave the garage door open a crack to keep from getting carbon monoxide poisoning. If we do, when the exhaust system heats, it'll turn the moisture in it and the surrounding air into water vapor, which will be seen coming from the garage. I don't know how high it'll billow into the air, but it will be noticeable to anyone passing the dacha."

"What's left?" Persik questioned, his teeth still chattering.

"These," Eka said, holding the stack of blankets that she found in the closet.

"That works," Persik conceded as he took one, "especially since we'll only be here a short time."

"Why a short time?" the junior consulate asked.

"The FSB has a reputation for efficiency," Persik answered as he wrapped himself in the blanket. "When they discover that we've left our Indonesian safehouse and they can't get a GPS location, they'll search every dacha in the area."

"How do you know?"

"Because that's what I'd do, and I'm only a Bali police lieutenant with a fraction of their resources."

Wayan agreed.

"How will you know when Doctor Kuzma is rescued," Eka asked the junior consulate.

"Tjay will call for our location."

"Let's hope he gets here soon," Olena added, everyone turning around and seeing her hand resting on an open book in the center of the desk.

"What were you looking at?" Eka asked as she joined her.

"This is a book on northwestern Russia and the adjoining Scandinavian countries. The map shows we're only five hundred fifty-five miles from Finland," Olena said, tracing her finger from Moscow to the Finnish city of Lappeenranta, which was twenty miles from the Russian border.

"Assuming your husband joins us, our presence in Moscow and his escape will mean tighter border security with every intelligence agency in the country searching for us. I don't know how we'd get into Finland."

"The same way we got here," she said, looking through the back window, pointing to the open field, and telling him her plan.

10

Nazarov received word that Kuzma had escaped from the hospital at six in the evening, twenty minutes after bursting into the Indonesian dacha. Because of this success and the rescue of Olena Kuzma, the FSB colonel understood that if he had any hope of catching the fugitives, he needed to act quickly. If they could orchestrate their escape from Oymyakon, return to Moscow, and extract Fedir Kuzma from the hospital, he wasn't going to bet against them getting themselves and those with them out of the country.

Because Moscow, with a population of seven million, had hundreds of thousands of dachas within an hour's drive of the city, not counting abandoned buildings and farmhouses, he believed that using a military drone with IR capabilities to overfly search area was the fastest way to find the fugitives. However, Lazarev sternly refused his request.

"If I ask the air force for a drone for domestic surveillance, the Defense Minister will ask why I need it," the general said. "I've used an extraordinary number of resources to kidnap Doctor Kuzma and his wife, set up his lab, and keep them prisoner while he completes his work. Only a few know about this. If they escape the country, the world will know that the Russian government kidnapped them and forced the doctor to work against his will in Moscow to keep his wife safe."

Nazarov knew that the general not asking for government resources outside the FSB meant he'd stepped deeper into the quicksand of being the fall guy.

"I'm getting hungry. Does Moscow have food delivery services?" Eka asked the junior consulate.

"There's quite a few. But there will be a significant delivery charge this far from the city." After saying this, he seemed to be lost in thought. When he came out of it, he said he knew a way to tell Tjay where they were without the FSB listening.

"How?" Wayan asked.

"Send him a message," the junior consulate said and explained that just as a food delivery service could bring something to them, a messenger service could deliver a note to the embassy.

The junior associate wrote the note to Tjay on a sheet of copy paper and put it inside an envelope he found on the desk. Within the message were the GPS coordinates of the dacha, which were taken from his satphone. Because the messenger company had an existing contract with the embassy, and their ultra-premium service was requested, meaning the messenger would make no other deliveries along the way, they immediately dispatched a driver.

"Let's hope Tjay gets this to the persons rescuing your husband from the hospital," Eka said.

"Assuming they're successful and get our new location, let's discuss timing," Wayan added. "We're here for the night because, as brilliant as Olena's idea was of how we escape, we need to wait for daylight to make it work. If Doctor Kuzma isn't here by then, and in the absence of information that leads us to believe he will be here, we'll assume the rescue failed and leave without him. From Tjay's warning, it sounded like the FSB was on its way to the embassy's dacha. That means they'll search the area, and it's only a matter of time until they find us here."

Olena said she agreed, saying it would be foolish to wait longer if they couldn't verify the rescue was successful.

The call from the Bratva lieutenant to the minivan driver occurred within minutes of Kuzma's transfer from the ambulance, instructing him to cruise around Moscow, taking a non-repetitive route to avoid suspicion, until he received a drop-off point for the doctor. Setting expectations, he said the drop-off location might not come for quite a few hours.

"The doctor is regaining consciousness now that we took him off his IV," the driver said. "He should be fine."

"Keep him healthy. There's a substantial fee for this delay, and we won't collect it if we deliver a body."

When the driver told the other soldiers they were driving around Moscow for an indeterminate number of hours until given a new dropoff location, there was an audible groan—all having counted on spending the evening at a local club with a bottle of vodka and hot women of ill repute.

"Water," Kuzma asked hoarsely.

The driver and soldier in the passenger seat beside him gave one another a questioning look, knowing there was none in the vehicle because they expected to drop him off quickly. Warned by the lieutenant to keep him healthy, they drove for another ten minutes before the driver saw a Shell Café in the distance. Knowing he could be driving around Moscow for some time, he decided to get everything done in one stop. He'd refuel on the gas side of the Shell parcel as one of his men went into the café to get bottles of water and sandwiches. While they were at it, they'd take advantage of the restroom, the three still dressed as hospital employees.

While the vehicle was being refueled and food and bottled water ordered at the café, the pseudo-patient told the driver that he needed to use the restroom.

"Take the doctor with you," he said.

Kuzma was unsteady as the pseudo-patient helped him out of his seat and onto the concrete covered by an inch of snow. As they walked the twenty yards to the men's room, the soldier's arm was tight around the doctor's waist. For whatever reason, he didn't give a second thought to the fact that Kuzma was walking in a thin pair of slippers and wearing a hospital gown with the back flapping open in the frigid weather exposing his butt to those at the station and anyone sitting at a table on the window side of the café. The driver, who was busy filling the vehicle with gas, was looking the other way and thinking about which route he would take through Moscow to avoid the treacherous traffic that choked parts of the city at this time of day. However, a half dozen people used their phones to capture the moment and put it on social media. Only when the pseudo-patient returned Kuzma to the vehicle did the driver, and the soldier returning with the food and water, notice Kuzma's attire and that he was the center of attention, with everyone pointing at him.

Sergei Lazarev was stunned at the video of Kuzma at the gas station but elated he was still in Moscow. What surprised him was that the gas station was on the opposite side of the city from the Indonesian embassy. If they were taking the doctor there, why not go straight from the hospital? The only explanation was that Kuzma was going to the Indonesian dacha, which was on the same side of the city as the gas station. But now that the fugitives had left, he was convinced he'd be taken to wherever they were hiding.

The general believed the common link in finding their new hiding place was Deputy Chief of Mission Tjay, who seemed to have his hand in everything the fugitives did. Therefore, needing him back in the game, he ordered the embassy's communications restored, that no one is prevented from entering the building, and routine surveillance is re-instituted. Now that they'd broken the embassy's most recent decryption keys, the Service of Special Communications and Information would prioritize the real-time decryption of their communications and data traffic, letting him receive this information at the same time as the Deputy Chief of Mission.

Sergei Burkov first learned of the incident at the Shell station when his lieutenant showed him the video on social media.

"How long ago did this happen?" he asked.

"Thirty minutes. But it's been viewed over a hundred thousand times."

"Idiots. I could see the vehicle's license plate number and the faces of our three men in the video. Exchange cars with those morons in a dead zone and ensure it has darkened windows so the city's surveillance cameras can't see inside.

"And Kuzma?

"We fulfilled our contract. Tell Tjay that he either takes delivery of the doctor now or I return him to the hospital."

Burkov's lieutenant arrived at the embassy and was escorted to the office of the Deputy Chief of Mission. His arrival solved a significant problem that confronted Tjay. Fifteen minutes ago, he received a written message from the junior consulate giving where he and the four fugitives relocated. His concern was how to tell Burkov, knowing the FSB had only returned his communications because they'd broken their encryption keys and could easily hear every conversation and read every data file.

Tjay spoke first before the lieutenant could deliver his ultimatum. "Here's where you'll bring the doctor," he said, handing him a slip of paper on which he'd written the coordinates.

"Where is this?"

"A dacha an hour east of here."

He took the paper and left without further comment.

Once Burkov's lieutenant knew where to bring Fedir Kuzma, he phoned the driver of the minivan and told them to go to a rest stop at the eastern edge of Moscow, a site they both knew, and wait there until he secured a vehicle into which they could transfer the doctor. Because the minivan had been the center of attention on social media when the gown-wearing, bare-butted Kuzma stepped out of it, he didn't want it transporting the doctor to the dacha, fearing the police would recognize the vehicle and follow it. Therefore, he told the minivan's driver to meet him at a rest stop at the eastern edge of Moscow, a site they both knew, and wait there while he brought another vehicle into which they could transfer Kuzma.

It took three hours for the lieutenant to get a Cadillac Escalade from a dealership the Bratva owned and arrive at the rest stop on the opposite side of the city. As the black Escalade parked in the space next to the minivan, the lieutenant watched its front and side doors open. Two soldiers then guided the hospital-gowned Kuzma out of the vehicle and into the open door of the Cadillac. However, just as the three soldiers in the minivan were about to change places with those in the Escalade, fate intervened.

The Moscow police, officially called the Main Directorate of Internal Affairs of the City of Moscow, is a part of the Ministry of Internal Affairs and comprises fifty thousand officers, with the Second Regiment responsible for patrol services. The two officers patrolling in their Lada Priora, a four-door compact, were ten-year veterans of the force, had been on duty for six hours, and were hungry. They went to their usual place for their dinner break—a rest stop in their patrol area with a Teremok fast food restaurant beside it, a chain that specialized in traditional

Russian dishes. Both officers were addicted to their blinis, a wheat pancake filled with caviar, fish, mushrooms, or potato.

The patrol car with two hungry police officers entered the rest stop's parking lot just as the hospital-gowned doctor was helped from the minivan into the Escalade. Because of his notoriety, caused by social media, they had a BOLO to look for the minivan. The officer in the passenger seat turned on the police car's flashing lights, hit the siren for a second to get the attention of the Escalade's driver, and pulled behind it. However, as they exited the Lada with their weapons drawn, the Escalade and minivan both left the parking lot, each going in separate directions.

The officers followed the Cadillac, the chase lasting only five minutes. The Escalade, holding the road better than the underpowered and lighter Lada, widened the distance between the vehicles and lost the two officers in the intertwining streets. By the time other police cruisers arrived to seal off the area, the Cadillac was speeding into the northern section of Moscow, pulling into the Cadillac dealership an hour later.

Because he knew the police would scour the eastern part of the city looking for the Cadillac, the lieutenant waited at the dealership for several hours before bringing him to the dacha. He thought by that time, after failing to find the Escalade, the police would call off their search believing it escaped their containment area.

At six that morning, with sunrise two hours and sixteen minutes away, Burkov's lieutenant exited the dealership in a white XT4, a Cadillac crossover, a vehicle significantly smaller than the Escalade.

Fedir Kuzma arrived at seven-thirty-five in the morning, forty-one minutes before sunrise. After a tearful reunion with his wife, Wayan went into the bedroom closet and got him clothing to replace the hospital gown and slippers.

"Our transport will be here in less than an hour," Wayan said, looking at his watch.

When Fedir returned from changing, everyone introduced themselves. Olena explained how Wayan, Eka, and Persik rescued her from Oymyakon and that Tjay arranged for his escape from the hospital. Fedir reciprocated by telling them what happened once he and Olena were separated in Sevastopol, Crimea.

"The Russians went through a lot of trouble to get you," Persik said. "They must have felt the technology you invented was so critical that they didn't want another nation to have it."

"My hardware is only marginally better than what they were developing."

"But they didn't know when they kidnapped you," Persik continued. "They believed, from what I was told, that you solved the problem of perceptual invisibility for a moving object."

"That assumption was only partially correct. They didn't understand how much my hardware was driven by software."

"But you didn't write the software; Olena did," Eka said. "We were told she has a doctorate in the science of crystals."

"Liquid crystal polymers," Olena corrected. "But I also have a doctorate in bionic AI."

"Where did you meet?"

"Fedir and I met at Kharkiv National University, where he received his doctorates."

"You both have more than one Ph.D.," Persik exclaimed.

"Mine are in systems engineering and material science," Fedir answered.

"I helped Fedir on the software portion of one of his projects, and we soon began dating. One thing led to another, and we got married."

"And you continued to collaborate," Eka said.

"Not officially," Olena replied. "He had branched out from traditional material science projects to the emerging field of camouflage technology. His work was recognized internationally as brilliant, and the government gave him the resources to continue it. When they moved Fedir to a lab at the National Academy of Sciences to keep his work secret, they allowed me to leave the government facility where I was employed and continue my work from our house."

"But, unknown to anyone but your husband, you wrote the software for his system."

"Those who the government assigned to write the software didn't fully understand my system and where I was taking it," Fedir said. "Olena did. We would talk about my work at home, and she knew what I was thinking and where I was going. At first, she wrote small routines, which I gave to those working on my software. Over time, those routines became larger and more sophisticated."

"And they believed you wrote it," Eka stated.

"In their eyes, I was a genius who could do anything. I eventually sent the software personnel to work at another government facility, with everyone believing I wrote my programs."

"When the Russians kidnapped you, did they take the equipment and software from your lab?" Wayan asked.

"They took the latest version of my hardware, which I had in a roller bag. The software was an older version. Olena was working on the update at home when they kidnapped us."

"But since they didn't know you wrote your husband's software, they never searched your house for it. They were there to kidnap you to give them leverage over Fedir," Wayan stated.

"That means the software is still in Ukraine," Persik said.

"I've had it the entire time," Olena corrected, removing a flash drive from the back of her belt buckle.

"Brilliant," Persik said. "And your husband periodically brought it to work to update his system."

Olena nodded in agreement.

"And that's the latest version of your software?" Wayan asked, looking at the flash drive in her hand.

"Yes, but I finished it after he left for work. It was never installed on his system."

"Then the hardware they took won't work without it," Persik said.

"This software update is extensive. It eliminates distortions caused by the camouflaged object's movement over uneven terrains, such as in the mountains, or on the beach or snow where heavy objects sink."

"My turn," Wayan said, recounting his team's experiences and the role that Tjay played in their rescue. "Do you have anything to add?" Wayan asked the junior consulate.

"If my understanding is correct in what you intend to do, I'm going to need to take a photo of each of you and get some information."

"What for?" Wayan asked.

The consulate told him.

"That's something I didn't consider," Wayan conceded.

The junior consulate had just gotten what he needed when the sound of an approaching plane pierced the air. It was eight-thirty.

The bright yellow Cessna 207 skiplane slowly descended and touched down a half mile behind the dacha, the nearest level patch of snow. When it stopped, Belevich stepped hard on his left brake pedal and pushed his throttle forward slightly, causing the aircraft to turn one hundred eighty degrees so that it was pointed down the same smooth strip of snow on which it landed. By the time he shut off the engine, five people were trudging through the snow toward the aircraft, the junior consulate looking at them from inside the dacha as he removed the phone from his pocket and called the embassy.

Although the aircraft appeared close, walking through the snow-covered, unevenly plowed field took time, especially for

Fedir Kuzma, who was still weak from his hospital stay. Ten minutes after they left the dacha, they were less than halfway to the aircraft.

Given his inability to obtain air force surveillance and detection equipment, Nazarov didn't believe he could find where the fugitives were hiding before they escaped. That belief changed early in the morning when, standing on the only hill in the area so that he could get an unobstructed view of what lay before him, he saw a bright yellow skiplane fly just above the treetops, which he knew was too low for radar to detect. Although skiplanes weren't an unusual sight outside Moscow in the winter, that the fugitives had escaped Omsk in one made him think they'd try to duplicate that means of escape from Moscow.

His position on the hill allowed him to see the plane's line of descent until it disappeared in the distance. Noting its direction, he ordered his men to return to their vehicles and follow the road to their right, which paralleled the aircraft's flight path. Because they parked a distance from the top of the steep snow-covered hill, it took ten minutes to return to the vehicles and get underway.

The dirt road they were on, which had three inches of fluffy snow covering it, hid the deep ruts created by farming equipment and made the going slow, Nazarov's two vehicles unable to go much over twenty-five mph. Thirty agonizing minutes after they started down it, the colonel saw the seaplane parked a mile away in a field ninety degrees from them with no visible road going there.

He considered going off-road and through the open area between him and the aircraft. However, not knowing what was beneath the snow-covered landscape, and because of the two long wire fences between them and the plane, he thought that decision was a recipe for disaster and continued down the rutted road hoping to find a turnoff. He found it a quarter of a mile later.

As Nazarov got closer to the plane, he saw that the road veered to the right and passed a hundred yards behind the tail of the aircraft, which had its prop turning and the doors closed. As the plane started moving, he yelled for his driver to stop and for his men to get out of the vehicles and shoot it down. With the aircraft rapidly accelerating, his men laid down heavy gunfire to bring down the skiplane, which quickly climbed, leveled out above the treetops, and faded into the distance. Unable to call the air force to shoot it down, he watched in frustration as the Kuzmas and the three Indonesian fugitives, who he assumed were on the plane, got away.

inland's eight-hundred-thirty-mile border with the Russian Federation is bucolic in appearance, consisting of extensive taiga forests intermixed with small cities, towns, and villages. The government protects this border with random patrols and sophisticated radar systems. However, one of the inherent limitations of even the most advanced system is that the height of the surrounding ground clutter governs the minimum altitude at which it can detect aircraft.

The yellow Cessna skiplane was flying at an altitude of one hundred fifty feet above the ground, approximately seventy feet above the treetops, and too low for border radar to detect. Belevich was familiar with this route, having previously used it to smuggle goods from Finland to Moscow. Therefore, he knew the location and height of radio and cell phone towers and other manufactured obstructions, adjusting his altitude to stay less than a hundred feet above them.

Before taking off for the dacha, Belevich changed the Cessna's tail number by covering the first two letters with similar lettering, changing it from RA, which designated the skiplane as a Russian aircraft, to OH, which identified it as Finnish. Therefore, when he requested permission to enter the airport control area and land on its snow strip, the tower assumed the plane was a domestic aircraft flying inter-country since it couldn't see on radar from what direction it came. As a result, customs and immigration weren't dispatched to ask for passports and a cargo manifest. Belevich would remove the lettering before returning to Russia.

Three and a half hours after leaving the field behind the dacha, the plane landed on a patch of snow at the Lappeenranta Airport, two and a half miles from the center of the city of seventy-two thousand. The patch was on the far side of the airport and created each winter so residents could receive and send essential goods if the airport and roads were closed to commercial traffic. The fact that contraband was sometimes loaded with this cargo on outbound planes was looked upon by the local authorities as an accommodation to the pilots, the thought being that it was Russia's problem since the goods ended up on their side of the border.

When Nazarov watched the Cessna 207 escape with the Kuzmas and the three Indonesians, he knew the only place it could go was Finland because neither the pilot nor the escapees were stupid enough to stay in the Russian Federation. Given the plane's size and his belief that the pilot wouldn't risk refueling in Russia, their destination had to be Lappeenranta, the nearest Finnish city. Incensed that they escaped, and aware he would be the fall guy, he racked his brain for a way to bring them back.

He'd been briefed that getting into Finland was easy, the FSBs intelligence division indicating that low-flying aircraft could enter their airspace without detection if it stayed below two hundred feet above the ground. Although the speed of single-engine aircraft varies widely because the engines could be significantly different, he'd been in a similar-sized Cessna that made the same engine sound, which likely meant it had a similar engine. The speed of that plane maxed out at two hundred mph. Assuming the same for the skiplane meant it would be in Lappeenranta in approximately three hours

Since he held the Kuzmas Ukrainian passports, and they needed one to leave the country in anything but a small radar-evading plane, he believed Tjay would have his counterpart at the Finnish embassy in Helsinki issue one to them, delivering them to the aircraft in Lappeenranta, along with anything else they required.

Nazarov's solution for stopping them from leaving Lappeenranta, assuming he was correct in predicting their destination, came to him when he juxtaposed his position with Finnish authorities who wanted to apprehend five fugitives who fled into Russia. Estimating he had three hours to pull his plan together, he began making calls.

The Indonesian embassy in Finland was in Helsinki, one hundred forty-three miles southwest of Lappeenranta and a two-hour fifty-six-minute drive via route six and the E75. Following his call with the junior consulate and the receipt of the data from him, Tjay phoned his embassy counterpart there and requested that the Kuzmas be issued Indonesian passports, and that the passports of the three accompanying them be given the proper entry and exit stamps. Although he knew the FSB would monitor the call, he had no choice because of the tight timing, believing Lazarev and those at Lubyanka would have difficulty initiating an operation in Finland so quickly to stop their departure.

"I have the stamps, but the ambassador will never allow me to remove them from the embassy. We use them more often than we care to admit. If something happens, they'll take time to replace, not to mention the diplomatic furor it will cause if they fall into the wrong hands."

Knowing his counterpart required an explanation along with the request, Tjay said that he couldn't disclose what the five had done, but that the Minister of Defense had conceived and sanctioned it. "Getting them to Jakarta is a national priority because, if they're caught, the discovery of those stamps will be a fart in the middle of a cyclone," he stated.

"Point taken. Let's not disappoint the Minister," his counterpart replied. "I'll have my assistant bring the passports. Three will be replacements, and two will be new."

"I'll send the names, photos, and other required information. They'll also need tickets to get them from Lappeenranta Airport to Jakarta as quickly as possible."

Thirty minutes after Tjay sent the information, he received a call from his counterpart's assistant saying he'd purchased the tickets online and that the passports would be ready in less than ten minutes, after which he'd deliver them to the Lappeenranta Airport. "How will I find them?" he asked.

"Look for a yellow skiplane."

Belevich was the last to disembark the Cessna, intending to find a fuel truck to refill his tanks and return to Russia. As he stepped onto the packed snow, a Volkswagen Transporter police van, followed by a government vehicle with two customs and immigration officials, pulled in front of the aircraft. The three police officers inside the van got out and stood beside their vehicle as the officials approached the six and asked for identification. Four presented passports. The Kuzmas couldn't.

"Everyone but him," an official said to the officers, pointing at Belevich.

They moved forward and handcuffed the five.

"What's this about?" Wayan asked in English since he didn't know either Finnish or Swedish, the two official languages of the country.

"The Russian police asked us to take you into custody. They're on their way here to return you to Moscow," one official stated.

"On what charges?"

"Escape from prison. But you already know that."

"It's a lie."

"You'll need to sort it out with them because you're being denied entry into the country."

"Isn't there an extradition process, and don't we have the right to a lawyer who can give our side of the story?" Eka asked.

"Finnish law allows for discretionary authority to extradite a suspect to a foreign state even if we don't have an international obligation to do so."

"At whose discretion?" Persik asked.

The official pointed to himself and his partner. "Officers, please take these five to the detention cells until the flight from Moscow arrives."

"What about him?" one officer asked, pointing to the pilot.

"They only gave us the five names," the other official answered. "As for you," he said, looking to Belevich. "If we didn't have a couple of hours of paperwork with these five, you'd also be gracing a cell for smuggling them into Finland. Peel those letters off your tail number and leave before we change our minds."

"I need gas."

"Refuel quickly," the first official stated.

When the assistant to the Finnish embassy's Deputy Chief of Mission arrived at the Cessna 207, he saw a fuel truck parked beside the aircraft and someone, who he assumed was the pilot, standing beside the person refueling the plane. The assistant introduced himself and asked where his passengers were.

"They've been arrested and are waiting for a Russian plane to bring them to Moscow," Belevich answered.

"When were they arrested?"

"Thirty minutes ago, and I'll be joining them if I don't get my aircraft out of Finland in a hurry."

The assistant phoned his Deputy Chief of Mission, who conferenced in Tjay. The assistant explained what the pilot said.

"They can't be allowed to return to Moscow," Tjay stated. "If they do, aside from the technology we'd lose, this will either be a diplomatic catastrophe, or the Russians'll blackmail us."

"Any ideas?" the counterpart asked.

"I do," Belevich, who was standing behind the assistant, interrupted. "You had the volume high enough so that I heard everything," the pilot explained.

"Put the call on speaker," Tjay said. "He got them here; maybe he has a way to get them out."

The assistant did as he was told and moved away from the Cessna so that the refueling tech, who was wearing AirPods, couldn't overhear.

"To be clear," Tjay explained, "we need to get them out of Finland and to another country where they can get on a flight to Jakarta. That means without the host government of that country believing they're fleeing fugitives and creating a diplomatic mess."

"I understand," the pilot responded calmly. "I can do that, but it will be very expensive because I'll lose my business and won't be able to return to Russia or enter Finland again."

"How expensive?"

Belevich told him.

"My contingency account and emergency funds are nearly drained. I can't come close to that number, even though I'd pay it if I had the money."

"To clarify, you said that the Minister of Defense initiated this mission?" Tjay's counterpart asked.

"That's correct."

"If we share the pain, we share the glory," he responded.

Tjay understood that to mean that if his counterpart paid the money, they were equal partners in the mission's success. He agreed.

"Once I leave, if there are unanticipated expenses associated with extracting everyone, I'll need a wire reimbursement," Belevich added. "I won't know what that is ahead of time."

"If it's within reason. Half the amount now and the rest when they're safe," the counterpart said to Belevich.

"Deal. If I fail, the money will not do me any good because I'll either be dead or in a Russian prison forever."

"Where do I wire the money?"

Belevich gave him the information. Fifteen minutes later, he confirmed receipt of the funds.

"I assume the Russians already know your name or soon will, given their resources. Therefore, given what you're undertaking, their intelligence networks will be looking for you. Russian intelligence is no joke, and they're excellent at finding someone. You'll need a new passport and identity. If you don't have one, we can help," Tjay stated.

"In my line of work, a change of identity now and then is a good thing. I have that covered," he responded with a smile, although only the associate could see it.

"What do you have planned?"

Belevich told him.

The airport had three holding cells behind an unmarked code-entry door next to baggage claim. Each was ten feet wide and ten feet deep, with gray concrete floors, walls, and ceilings, with only a stainless steel toilet and metal bunk bed within. Because the jail was designed to hold persons until they could be taken by local authorities to the central jail or placed on an aircraft with a law enforcement officer, they were minimalistic. Eka and Olena were in one cell, Wayan and Persik in another, and Fedir Kuzma in the last. Prior to entering the cell, their possessions and belts were confiscated, and they were denied a phone call. When Wayan asked why, he was told the call was useless since there was no legal way to stop this extradition, and they would soon be the Russians' problem and could ask them once they reached Moscow.

"Thank you for trying to rescue us," Olena said to Eka as the two sat on the metal bunk and looked at the gray wall beyond the metal bars. "I know it's going to be bad for you and your friends. Are you and Wayan married?" she asked, keeping her voice low so those in the other cells couldn't hear.

"We're not married or engaged. We live together and are getting to know each other."

"I can see in his eyes how much he cares about you. He seems a person of good character with a strong sense of what is right. He's also handsome, with doesn't hurt."

They both laughed.

"Part of the joy of partnering with someone is experiencing life together as you grow older," she said, talking about her and Fedir for several minutes before Eka changed the subject.

"What will they do to you and your husband when they get you back?"

"Increase security and bleed us dry of everything we know. They'll never let us return home or be free because we know too much about the technology and would tell the world they kidnapped us to get it."

"You would have had a better life in Bali."

"Better because of the climate, but otherwise the same," Olena said, surprising Eka with that statement.

"You wouldn't be a prisoner."

"That depends on your definition. Your government would place us in a very secure location because of the nature of our work and guard us 24/7, so we couldn't communicate with another foreign power or be kidnapped again. As I said, the only change is the climate."

"Living in a gilded cage," Eka stated.

"But a nicer cage than the Russians have planned for us."

"The Russians may not be as restrictive with you since they don't know you're the software genius behind your husband's hardware."

"They will when their software engineers speak with Fedir."

"If you could leave this cell and do anything you wanted, what would it be?"

"A farmer growing flowers, grains, herbs, and anything else the earth allowed me to harvest."

Eka said that was the last profession she would have guessed.

"Ukrainians and Russians aren't that different because we respect and love what comes from the earth. If it were summer, you'd see that every Russian dacha or Ukrainian household has a garden growing vegetables, flowers, herbs, and so forth. It's part of our culture and something we've done from the time we were children. Fedir and I had a large garden in Ukraine."

"Maybe they'll give you a house. They'll want to keep you happy and motivated."

"The Russians use the stick more than the carrot, if you know what I mean. Going back to what I said earlier, I'm worried about the three of you. We're both valuable and a liability to the FSB. I'm sure you know what will happen once they bring you to Moscow and finish their interrogations."

Eka said she did.

12

The Antonov AN-24 landed at the Lappeenranta Airport at four in the afternoon, three hours and fifteen minutes after Wayan, Eka, Persik, and the Kuzmas were arrested. Five people were on the plane—two pilots, Nazarov, and two FSB soldiers. While the crew remained onboard, everyone else disembarked down the stairway brought to their aircraft. At the bottom were two airport police officers, who introduced themselves and drove them to baggage claim.

Immediately, the three saw all eyes staring at them. There were several reasons for this. The first was that eighty percent of Finland's native-born population had blonde hair, and eighty-nine percent had blue eyes. The three Russians had black hair, black eyes, and dark stubble on their faces. The second was that they wore a white shirt, a black suit with a monochromatic tie, and a black parka—standard FSB winter attire when not in uniform. This identified them as Russians, especially since the small Finnish city's leading employers were lumber mills, lime and cement factories, and machine shops. Subsequently, everyone dressed casually. The airport police, seeing the increased attention with people using their cellphones to video the group, hurried them to the access door, entered the code, and brought them to the holding cell area. They then left Nazarov and his men alone with the prisoners while they went down the hall to generate the paperwork that needed to be signed.

This was the first time Nazarov had seen them in person, previously having photos of the five prisoners and only recently receiving the summary background dossiers given to him by Lazarev.

He silently looked at the faces of those who'd eluded him for so long. "Let me introduce myself," he said, breaking the silence. "I'm Colonel Stasik Nazarov of the FSB," he said, walking along the cells and initiating eye contact with Wayan, Persik, and Eka. I look forward to escorting you to Lubyanka and discovering more about this unsuccessful adventure."

"How did you find us? Olena asked.

"We intercepted the Indonesian embassy's communications. A motley group. Gunter Wayan," he continued, looking at him through the cell bars. "A disgraced Indonesian police officer turned private investigator. That demotion must have been hard to take. That necessitates me asking how a person of such low accomplishment rescue Fedir and Olena Kuzma?"

"It was easy given the Russian government's, and I'm sure your, gross incompetence," Wayan replied, erasing the smug look from the colonel's face.

"Suton Persik," he continued, ignoring the taunt. "A detective in the Bali police department. This is what happens when you get in over your head and challenge the FSB."

"As Wayan implied, competing with the FSB wasn't much of a challenge. They're overrated. If a private investigator and detective can embarrass you on your home turf, it's no wonder you do so poorly against the Americans."

That remark almost caused the pot to boil over, but Nazarov controlled his temper and kept his facial expression neutral. He'd make Wayan and Persik wish they'd never uttered those remarks when he got them into an interrogation room. He was about to menace Eka when the officers returned with the paperwork and turned his attention to them.

The FSB colonel signed the five presented forms, after which each prisoner was taken from their cell, handcuffed, and marched through the baggage claim terminal to the waiting van. Nazarov escorted Wayan.

"We'll see how long that defiance lasts when you're at Lubyanka," the colonel said. "The rumors you may have heard about our interrogations aren't close to what you'll experience. You'll beg me to put a bullet in your head."

When the van pulled in front of the aircraft stairs, Nazarov asked the officers to remove the prisoner's handcuffs.

"Don't you want to keep them on until they're in their seats?" one officer asked, offering the cuffs to Nazarov.

"We have flex cuffs onboard," he responded, drawing a nod from the officers who took that as a sign they weren't invited onboard and left.

The women were the first to board, one soldier standing behind Eka and Olena as he ushered them onboard. Kuzma and Persik were next, the second soldier similarly marching them up the stairway. Wayan and Nazarov were the last to go up the stairway. The colonel didn't expect any trouble from his prisoners because there was nowhere to run. Beside the tarmac on which the AN-24 was parked, there was a hard-packed snow runway. Fifteen hundred feet beyond that was the main runway. In the opposite direction, barren, snow-covered ground extended a mile to the eight-foot-high perimeter barbed wire security fence.

Entering the aircraft, Nazarov expected to see his soldiers cuffing the prisoners to their seats. Instead, he saw two soldiers lying unconscious on the floor with the prisoners standing behind them. That was the last thing he'd remember before someone dressed in white workman's overalls, with the chevron of an aviation fuel company on the front, hit him on the side of the head with a blackjack—a molded lead bludgeoning device. The two pilots had been similarly bludgeoned that person, who came aboard to inquire how much fuel they required.

"Nice overalls," Wayan said.

"Gucci should make them for what I had to pay the fuel service operator for them," Belevich responded.

"I thought the officials told you to leave as soon as you fueled," Wayan said, disbelieving he was still in Lappeenranta.

"I have an engine problem. Since the airline mechanics at this airport know little about small planes and only have maintenance manuals and service experience for larger aircraft, they told me to stay here until they could get a certified mechanic to look at it. That was hours ago."

"Do you know what happened to the embassy official?" Eka asked.

"When I told him what I was going to do, he didn't want any part of it. Instead, he left these," he said, removing five passports from his pocket.

"How do we get out of here if your plane's broken?" Wayan asked.

"It just needs a part," he answered, removing it from his pocket and holding it between his fingers.

Prior to leaving the FSB's aircraft, they used flex cuffs to tie up the pilots, soldiers, and the colonel. They then went to Belevich's plane, which was in a nearby hangar because the airport's protocol called for any aircraft that required maintenance to be in a hangar until a tech could diagnose the problem and fix it or order the parts.

It took two minutes for Belevich to replace the missing part and five to tow the aircraft to the end of the snow runway. The engine started cleanly, and it took off sixty seconds later, maintaining a low altitude as it headed northwest.

"Not that I'm ungrateful," Wayan said, unfastening his seat belt and leaning forward into the cockpit, "but where are we going?"

"To the island of Öja, three hundred miles from here."

"And from there?"

"You'll see."

With sunset occurring at four forty-three pm, it was dark when Nazarov awoke thirty minutes after being struck in the head. Seeing that the soldiers beside him were still unconscious, he grabbed the seat beside him and pulled himself to his feet, staggering to the first aid kit clipped to the bulkhead behind the cockpit. After removing two ammonia capsules, he revived the soldiers and cockpit crew.

Although he didn't see who hit him, his money was on the skiplane pilot, the only person with the opportunity and means to help the five fugitives escape. As the soldiers and crew were starting to pull it together and regain their equilibrium, he heard the two officers who'd escorted the prisoners to the aircraft calling him from the metal stairway, the shaking of the stairs indicating they were coming up it. Running to the door, he barely got there to block their way before they came on board.

"Is everything alright?" one officer asked.

"We delayed our departure to ensure we had the proper arrangements for our prisoners in Moscow," the colonel answered, giving them the first excuse that came to mind.

"Would you like us to return them to their holding cells?"

"Give us five or ten minutes and we'll be on our way. Thank you for your professionalism in checking back with me. I'll write a letter of commendation when I return to Moscow."

The officers, happy with his response, went to their vehicle and left.

Nazarov walked into the cockpit. "Call the tower and ask if they know where the yellow skiplane went that was here when we arrived," he ordered.

The co-pilot asked, receiving a response that the controller saw it departing to the northwest.

"That's toward the other coast and in the direction of Sweden. Stockholm is only four hundred miles from here," the colonel stated, having looked at the area's geography on the flight from Moscow.

"Unless he has a good aeronautical map or program giving the location of obstructions like radio towers, it's dangerous flying VFR at night," the pilot interjected.

"How will he navigate?" Nazarov asked.

"An aeronautical chart will give him the frequencies for navigational aids along his flight route. If he has the chart, he won't get lost," the pilot explained.

"I don't care if they're headed to Sweden or another city in Finland. Wherever they're going, so are we." The colonel looked at his watch. "Assuming they have a forty-five minute to an hour lead, how long will it take to catch them?" he asked the pilot.

The pilot wanted to say that he had no idea what heading the skiplane was on when it left, and even if he did, the pilot could change it multiple times by locking onto various navigational aids to get to a destination only he and his passengers knew. However, realizing the colonel was stressed and didn't want to hear that they had a snowball's chance in hell of finding the skiplane, which wasn't the best career move, he avoided a discussion of direction. "We're faster than the Cessna," he responded instead. "Because it's dark, we'll see them from quite a distance. But..."

Nazarov cut him off. "Then get this plane in the air and keep your speed at the maximum, or tomorrow you both will be flying planes in the Antarctic."

The pilot and co-pilot believed the colonel and, therefore, omitted giving him a critical piece of information. After summoning the ground crew to remove the stairway, the pilot asked the tower for an expedited takeoff, which was granted. The flight crew rapidly went through their takeoff checklist with worried looks on their faces because, before being cut off by the colonel, the pilot was about to tell him that pushing the engines to the max consumed an extraordinary amount of fuel and they'd run the tanks dry in about two hours. If that happened, they believed the chance of successfully crash-landing a plane in the dark in Finland was infinitesimally slight because of the large number of forests, hills, and other obstructions that would remain unseen in an uncontrolled descent until impact.

"What's the holdup?" Nazarov yelled from the back.

With that question, the pilot turned on his landing lights, pushed the throttles forward, and headed for the runway.

At six twenty in the evening, an hour and forty-five minutes after leaving Lappeenranta, the skiplane landed on the hardpacked ice of Bothnia Bay, the northern part of the Gulf of Bothnia. The rectangle of ice on which it set down was bordered by small fires, thirty miles from the *island of Öja and the eight-hundred-person village with the same name. Belevich was familiar with the village because many of its residents were smugglers. He'd landed on* Bothnia Bay *many times to load or offload smuggled goods, flying into and out of Russia, Finland, and other Scandinavian countries.*

He'd phoned one of his contacts on the island while in flight and told them the approximate time he'd land, requesting he create a landing strip—something they'd done in the past when smuggling goods onto or out of Finland at night. Because he'd asked for the makeshift runway to be thirty miles from the island, significantly farther than usual, he explained what he intended to do.

"Is there some reason you landed in the middle of nowhere?" Persik asked as Wayan climbed out of the aircraft and helped Eka onto the ice. However, their isolation dissipated minutes later with the roar of snowmobiles and the six pairs of lights that accompanied it.

When the snowmobiles came into view, they dispersed and put out the fires that bordered the landing strip. As they did, Belevich took four, five-gallon containers of aviation fuel from the rear storage compartment and began dousing the aircraft and the area beneath and around it.

"I hope you're not doing what I think you're about to do," Wayan said as Belevich threw three empty gas containers under the plane.

"Move a hundred yards away," was the pilot's only response as he took the half-empty container in his hand and laid a trail of avgas away from the skiplane. Stopping twenty yards from the Cessna, he struck his lighter, threw it on the line of gas that led to it, and began running in the opposite direction. Seconds later, the aircraft exploded, throwing wreckage in every direction and creating a raging fire in the spot where it had been.

"Are you crazy? Why did you do that?" Eka asked.

"I'm saving our lives. Do you believe the person who came after you in Lappeenranta will return to Russia and tell his boss that six civilians overpowered his team and escaped? You don't understand how these people think. You embarrassed him, and it's now personal. He'll follow us to the ends of the earth because we've more than likely screwed his career and made him look like a fool. He'll want revenge."

"This is to make him think our plane crashed," Wayan stated.

"I know this area extremely well. We're thirty miles from the island, and there's a strong current beneath us. Therefore, the ice here is thinner than you'll find closer to shore. The intense heat from the fire will melt through it and create a hole. With the wreckage strewn around, he'll believe our bodies are under the ice."

"If he chased us in this direction," Persik added. "Because you flew below radar, and it's dark, how could he follow us here?"

"There's only one person he can ask who knows the direction we left—the tower controller. They'll tell him we flew northwest. That indicates we're staying in-country, which is logical because we'd contend with customs and immigration if we flew south to Estonia or west into Sweden. And we certainly aren't going east and returning to Russia," Belevich said in a confident tone.

"He may not have been able to follow us here because," Persik said. "if I'm correct, northwest is a direction, not a heading. A few degrees difference in a course can mean hundreds of miles."

"You're right. However, because there are only small towns when flying across Finland on a northwest heading from Lappeenranta, this darkness means that the fire from the burning aircraft can be seen from some distance away, much like I saw the fires outlining our landing strip when I was twenty miles from it."

"Twenty miles isn't far," Persik continued.

"That's if they're flying below radar at two hundred feet. Unlike us, the Russian aircraft doesn't need to stay below radar. They can fly at a higher altitude, making their aircraft more fuel-efficient and giving them greater visibility. At five thousand feet, which is considered low, the pilot can see this fire from one hundred miles away, two-thirds of the distance from Lappeenranta here. That mileage increases with altitude."

"If I have this right, because his plane has two engines, it flies faster and higher than us. It wouldn't take him long at all to see this fire."

"You have it."

"The FSBs belief that we're dead might come true if we stand any longer on this sea of ice, slowly freezing to death," Eka commented, shivering as she did.

"Let's get you warm," Belevich said, herding the fugitives toward the snowmobiles, taking from one a snowsuit and helmet that was in the bag strapped to the back of the two-person vehicle. Belevich motioned the others to get their suits and helmets from the remaining vehicles.

"The snowmobiles will bring us to the mainland town of Kokkola, which is seven miles from here. It'll take ten minutes for us to get there and another fifteen to arrive at the airport," Belevich said.

"There's an airport that close to us?" Fedir asked.

"Only a few commercial flights go out of there daily, and we're not taking one. Instead, we're going to the general aviation terminal," Belevich said without further explanation as he donned his gear.

Although none of the snowmobile suits fit, they kept everyone warm during their ride to the Kokkola-Pietarsaari Airport, where Belevich and the five fugitives were dropped off in front of the general aviation terminal, two hundred yards beyond the main terminal. As the smuggler entered, a burly man with a heavy black beard greeted him. The two gave each other a bear hug and spoke for a few minutes in Russian. After their conversation, the burly man asked that everyone follow him outside.

When they opened the rear door of the terminal and walked onto the tarmac, they saw a Cessna Grand Caravan, a fourteen-passenger single-engine turboprop with a range of a thousand miles and a maximum speed of two hundred twelve mph, parked a dozen yards away.

Nazarov spoke with the pilot, and there was a problem of his own making. In his haste to get out of the Lappeenranta Airport and chase the fugitive's skiplane, threatening the crew with duty in the Antarctic if they didn't immediately get the AN-24 into the air and push its throttles to the max, he cut the pilot off before he could say that he wanted to refuel first. That was a mistake. He was accustomed to threatening others to get his way, which always worked because those he bullied knew the FSB could do whatever it wanted. However, in this situation, the result of this unquestioning obedience was that the aircraft was over northwest Finland and getting low on fuel.

"We can refuel at the Kokkola-Pietarsaari Airport, which is thirty minutes away," the pilot said. "If we go past it, we'll run out of gas and crash ten minutes later."

Knowing that he didn't have a choice, Nazarov told him to turn toward the airport and refuel. It was seven-ten pm, one hour fifty-five minutes after their departure from Lappeenranta.

Nazarov returned to his seat believing that he'd lost the fugitives and they could be anywhere, possibly not even in Finland. Looking out the window, he saw a pulsating glow on the horizon and returned to the cockpit. "What's that?" he asked the pilot, pointing to the light.

"That's what a fire looks like at night from the air," the pilot answered. "It appears less than a hundred miles ahead and toward Bothnia Bay and the airport. We'll get a close look at it shortly."

Less than half an hour later, Nazarov's plane approached the aircraft fire, which had diminished to a fraction of its original brilliance.

"That's too small to be a forest fire. Get closer; I want to see what's burning," the colonel ordered.

The pilot banked the plane and circled the fire, low enough for everyone to see the blackened hole in the ice with the wreckage strewn around it. There was no mistaking the bright yellow wings ripped off the Cessna.

"What happened?" Nazarov asked.

"It could be anything, from equipment or instrument failure to pilot error. They didn't run out of fuel because that's what exploded, blowing the aircraft apart and burning a hole in the ice."

"I want a closer look. Go lower," he demanded.

"I'm at minimal power, and we have five minutes of fuel, at most, before we won't make the airport," the pilot responded, banking to the left and putting the AN-24 into a wide descending spiral so that Nazarov could see out the window.

"Where are the bodies?" Nazarov questioned.

"Below the ice with the fuselage," the pilot offered.

"What about the snowmobile tracks?"

"A rescue party from either the mainland or that island," the pilot said, pointing to a lighted spec in the distance.

"If it's from the mainland, the tracks would run only to the wreckage and back, with or without survivors. If from the island, they would run to and from the island if there are no survivors but go to the mainland if there were since this postage stamp of an island likely doesn't have a hospital."

"That makes sense," the pilot said.

"Therefore, they're either at a mainland hospital, in their morgue, or as you suggested, under the ice. Do you want to know what I think?"

The pilot didn't want to say he didn't care because they were close to becoming a very heavy glider."

"The fugitives had these snowmobiles meet them and blew up their plane so that everyone would believe they perished in the crash," Nazarov said.

"And where would the snowmobiles take them?" the pilot asked.

"The same place we're going—the airport."

The pilot used that remark as his ticket to turn for the airport. Running on fumes, he set the plane down five minutes later at the Kokkola-Pietarsaari Airport, taxiing on one engine to the general aviation terminal because the other stopped inflight from a lack of fuel.

The plane taxied to a stop beside the fuel pumping station, where the pilot shut down his remaining engine, although it would have stopped on its own in another ten seconds. Looking out the window as they waited for someone to bring a stairway, Nazarov saw the Cessna Grand Caravan start its engine and its chocks being pulled. The aircraft's interior was well-lit because everyone within seemed to have their overhead light on. As the plane slowly left the terminal, Nazarov saw the faces of Wayan,

Olena Kuzma, and Persik in the windows of the taxiing aircraft. They were returning his stare.

"Ram that plane. Don't let it leave," Nazarov screamed at the pilot, who raised his hands in a gesture of helplessness, replying that they were out of fuel. Less than thirty seconds later, he saw the lights from the Cessna speeding down the runway.

13

"**Y**ou were right," Wayan said to Belevich, "he won't give up."

"Now that he's found us, it won't take long for him to be after us again," Belevich replied.

"We'll be difficult to follow flying at low altitude and in the dark," Persik commented.

"Yet, he somehow managed to find us. I don't expect that ability will change."

"Thanks to him, the Finnish police believe we're fugitives the Russian government wants for unspecified crimes. That's how we'll be categorized in their computer system," Wayan added. "If he discovers where we're going, he'll have the authorities arrest and hold us."

"On that subject, where are we going?" Eka asked Belevich.

"Two hundred eighty miles south of here to the thirteenth-century city of Turku, where someone I know will make you each a passport because the ones you have are flagged. As Wayan said, you're criminals in the Finnish computer system."

"And once we have the new passports?"

"I'll arrange for everyone to get to Jakarta."

"Purchasing forged passports and getting us out of the country takes a great deal of money. We don't have any," Wayan said.

"That problem has been solved," Belevich replied, recalling his conversation with Tjay's counterpart regarding ancillary expenses.

Wayan, knowing Belevich's inventiveness, didn't ask for details.

"How long will it take to get the passports?" Eka asked.

"You'll each have a passport and a package of identifications, which includes a driver's license and credit card, before morning."

"The police took our photos. If the facility where we exit the country has facial recognition software, alarms will sound because they'll link our faces our old passports," Persik warned.

"I'm sure this technology is prevalent in Indonesia. However, from experience, I can tell you that while Finnish Police and Customs have this technology, it's in its infancy because their citizens are suspicious about losing their privacy and afraid that Big Brother will constantly watch them. Therefore, Finland doesn't yet have large-scale automatic facial recognition."

"And we'll leave the country from Turku?" Wayan asked.

"Yes. The flight from Turku will take you to Rome, where you'll have a two-hour layover before continuing to Jakarta."

The five fugitives relaxed, and there was no further conversation until the Grand Caravan landed at the Turku Airport at nine pm. The plane taxied to the general aviation area, and as it was being refueled, Belevich's friend pulled beside it in a passenger van.

The friend took everyone, except the Grand Caravan pilot, to his workshop, which was twenty minutes away. After taking headshots of the five fugitives, he created new passports, each bearing an entry stamp for Finland. Belevich, who already had a forged passport, had an entry stamp placed on it. The Kuzmas were Estonian, their accent and facial features very similar to the citizens of that country. Wayan, Eka, and Persik were from India.

"Before you leave, I need three more things from you," the forger said, opening a drawer and removing a pair of scissors, a fingerprint card, and a sterile syringe.

They returned to the airport two hours later. As they passed the general aviation section on their way to the airport's main terminal, they saw a flurry of activity on the tarmac. Not only hadn't the Cessna departed as they expected, but police surrounded it, and the pilot was in handcuffs with Nazarov and his two soldiers beside him.

"You were right when you predicted he'd find us," Wayan said to Belevich. "But how did he do it so quickly?" He told the forger to pull the van to the road so they could see what was happening. He did and turned off the vehicle's lights.

"This is only a guess, but I'd say he wrote down or remembered the tail number of our plane. With that, he could ask Kokkola's tower to see if another airport in the system recorded our landing," Belevich said.

"He then called ahead to the Turku Airport police and had them arrest the pilot and anyone else on the plane," Wayan added, Belevich saying that was also his belief.

"I didn't know the tower recorded the tail numbers of private planes," Persik said.

"They do if you land on their runway because you need permission to land. A skiplane runway is temporary because it melts in warm weather and usually doesn't merit their attention. The tower will let us come and go without bother as long as we don't interfere with runway traffic," Belevich said.

"Did Nazarov use your tail number to track us to Lappeenranta?" Eka asked.

"He couldn't because I changed the first two letters before I landed and picked everyone up. I think he found us because it was the nearest foreign airport within range of my skiplane."

"It seems risky to take a commercial flight out of Turku, given Nazarov is here and speaking with police," Wayan said to Belevich, who nodded in agreement. "Is there a plan C for getting us out of the country?"

"There is, but first, we have to finish Plan B."

"We do?"

"You've got nothing," Lazarev told Nazarov after hearing the colonel's summary of what occurred from when he landed at Lappeenranta to his arrival at the Turku Airport. "You've put your foot in it with Finnish authorities by demanding the arrest of the pilot, a Finnish citizen who had every right to land his plane at that airport."

"I saw the fugitives on his plane when it left Kokkola."

"Did anyone see them get off the plane in Turku?"

"The police arrived ten minutes after the plane landed but only saw the pilot."

"Then, you've got nothing," the four-star repeated, his voice raised in irritation. "Let me summarize the diplomatic problems you've created. You were in Finland on the pretext of chasing fugitives fleeing justice. The police did us the diplomatic courtesy of arresting and holding them until you arrived. They deliver the fugitives to your aircraft, they escape, but you tell them they're onboard. Instead of returning to Moscow, you chase them across their country and land in two more cities."

"I couldn't let them get away," Nazarov defiantly responded.

"I told you to keep their escape low profile so that other government agencies and our president don't learn of your gross incompetence," Lazarev asserted.

With that statement, Nazarov noted that his boss once again reiterated that he was the fall guy.

"I'm aware that our country needs this technology, and the West will have it if the Kuzma's escape. These Indonesians don't have the right to kidnap people in our country."

"A violation of human rights we have in common with them," the four-star responded, brushing aside the statement.

"What are my orders?" the colonel asked. The question, posed in military parlance, was an attempt to shift future liability onto the general's shoulders."

"Call the Turku police and say you were mistaken, apologize to everyone, and tell the pilot we'll compensate him for this misunderstanding if he forgets it happened," Lazarev said.

There was an uneasy pause, broken when Nazarov asked the four-star if he had any suggestions on how to find the fugitives.

"They were at the airport because they wanted to leave the country. Assume they have new identities. Have our techs hack into the passenger manifests of airlines at nearby airports with departing flights. Most of them operate in Russia, and we already know how to get into their computers."

"We don't know their aliases."

"Three men and two women, with the possibility of a fourth man if the pilot accompanies them, traveling to the same destination. Start there."

"Looking at airlines in Turku first?" the colonel asked.

"Only if they're stupid, which they've disproven more than once. They'll assume you've shown the police their photos."

Nazarov was silent.

"I'd fly from Tallinn, Estonia, and possibly Helsinki because they're the closest airports, enabling me to get out of the area quickly. Look at long-haul charters; I wouldn't put that past them."

"Why not take a merchant vessel?"

"It would take too long to get to where they were going giving us more time to find them. One last thing," Lazarev continued. "You're not allowed to hijack or shoot down their plane. I want no publicity."

"Understood. I'm taking a more personal approach."

As Nazarov spoke with his boss, the forger who created fugitive's passports went to the city morgue. He and the medical examiner were close friends who brokered each other's services. In this situation, the forger needed two bodies, a male and a female. As the morgue often had unclaimed homeless, the city's policy was to have them cremated but keep the deceased's blood, hair samples, and fingerprints. The forger had taken all three means of identification from the Kuzmas and gave them to the medical examiner, who selected a male and female body listed as Matti Meikäläinen and Maija Meikäläinen, the English equivalent of John and Jane Doe. He then took the Kuzma's fingerprint cards and, at the forger's request, entered them into the national database and those of neighboring countries, including the Russian Federation, requesting information on their identities.

The FSBs division of fingerprints and biometrics received fifty thousand fingerprint submissions per week, sent in either an electronic or paper format. Government agencies received priority, with searches automatically made by sophisticated algorithms which accessed a network of databases and seamlessly sent results to the person or agency asking for the search, no person having laid eyes on the request or results. The exception to this automation was national security. Those search results were forwarded to the officer in charge of the fingerprint and biometric division, who would then call the relevant person or agency with the results.

When the request from Turku's medical examiner was received, it went to the bottom of the pile because it came from a civil agency in another country. For the next six hours, it languished as priority requests pushed it aside until, during a lull in activity, the algorithms were finally able to analyze the prints.

Because the results of this search contained names designated *Of Special Importance*, the country's highest security classification, denoting that release of this information would cause damage to the entire Russian Federation, they were forwarded to the division's officer in charge, along with the name of the individual to be contacted, General Viktor Lazarev.

As the officer in charge was in the same building, he requested a meeting, sitting in front of the general five minutes later and presenting the search results showing that the prints sent by the medical examiner belonged to Fedir and Olena Kuzma.

"Could they have faked the prints?" the general asked.

"Faking prints is difficult, but it's been done. This request was accompanied by an offer to send hair and blood samples. Therefore, I'd say the prints are authentic."

The general knew he couldn't ask for the samples or confirm the prints. That was tantamount to admitting he kidnapped the couple.

"Tell the medical examiner the prints are not in our database."

After the officer in charge left his office, he called Nazarov.

"The Kuzma's are dead," he said, explaining what he was told.

"How did they die?"

"It's not a question we can ask after responding that the fingerprints were not in our system."

"Why query the Russian Federation for the prints?"

"It's not the first fingerprint request we've received from Finland. It frequently happens when the unidentified deceased looks Russian."

"The timing of their deaths is too convenient, especially since the other fugitives aren't included in the search request."

"The three Indonesians hardly look Russian," Lazarev countered. "However, I share your pessimism, especially given the creativity of the fugitives in avoiding capture. They're considered alive until proven otherwise."

Finland is the only country where every port freezes in the winter. However, because three-quarters of the country's imports and ninety percent of their exports are by sea, keeping them open in the winter is vital to the economy. Therefore, icebreakers created lanes allowing ships access to the open waters of the Gulf of Finland and the Baltic Sea. These ice lanes can remain open for several days. The time they're navigable before the icebreakers are again needed depends upon the wind, storms, and other conditions that affect the reformation of the ice.

Belevich's Plan C was to drive the one hundred miles from Turku to Helsinki and take the ferry to the Tallinn, Estonia marine terminal, which was several miles from the country's largest airport. The ferry continued to operate in the winter despite the Gulf of Finland freezing over, using one of the ice lanes to transit between countries.

The van drove the five fugitives to the port, where Belevich purchased ferry tickets for the two-hour ride to Tallinn. To give validity to their cover story of being tourists, and because it would be suspicious to travel without luggage, each used their credit card at the Helsinki marine terminal to buy a carry-on bag, clothing, and personal items. They passed through Finnish customs and immigration without a second look from officials and received the same lack of concern when entering Estonia.

"Your forger knows his trade," Wayan said to Belevich as the six walked toward the taxi stand.

"He's expensive but, as you can see, extremely reliable."

"When does our flight to Jakarta leave, and how long is it?" Persik asked, having forgotten what Belevich told them when he booked the tickets online.

"We leave for Frankfurt, Germany, in three hours, have a fourteen-hour layover in Singapore, and if the flights are on time, arrive thirty-six hours from now."

"Got it," Persik said.

"You're sure you want to come with us?" Eka asked Belevich, learning on the ferry ride the Russian would accompany them to Indonesia. "It doesn't snow in Indonesia. We only have floatplanes and seaplanes."

"I'm only staying until I figure out what I want to do next. My Serbian passport lets me enter without a visa and stay for thirty days. That's long enough."

The taxi ride to the international airport took ten minutes, and after showing their passports at the ticket counter, each was issued their boarding passes. Wayan didn't alert Tjay or the Minister of Defense about their return because he didn't want anyone meeting them at the Jakarta airport and seeing the Kuzmas. Neither knew the names they were traveling under, which gave Fedir and Olena time to continue to their next destination without being noticed. The chink in the armor was that Wayan, Eka, and Persik's faces were in the country's facial recognition system, meaning they'd be stopped when their new passport names didn't match the name associated with their faces. That's when Wayan decided he'd call the Minister of Defense and tell him they'd arrived.

The six proceeded from the ticket counter to customs and immigration, passing through security, and walking to the departure gate and onto the plane without issue.

14

The six fugitives landed in Jakarta at midnight, ten days after Wayan, Eka, and Persik set foot in Moscow. After deplaning and with immigration control in front of them, they said their goodbyes. There were no smiles. Their experiences bonded them into a family, and they were sad it might be some time until they could see one another again.

The Kuzmas and Belevich passed through immigration without incident and began walking to the domestic departure terminal, a trek from the international concourse, where they'd purchase tickets for their seven-hundred-fifty-six-mile flight to the archipelago of Sumbawa. Wayan had called Captain Bakti Nabar from Germany and arranged for him to meet the trio at the Sumbawa airport and bring them to his family's sandalwood farm, which he inherited more than a year ago from his father.

Sandalwood is one of the most expensive trees in the world, each kilogram, or thirty-five ounces, selling for twenty thousand dollars. Nabar could have made a very good living running the farm but chose to remain a professional soldier. As a martial arts instructor and team member of the Kopassus, the Indonesian army's special forces group, he loved the challenge of military life and the opportunity to protect his country. Therefore, he paid his neighbors to tend to the trees, which had to be a minimum of fifteen years old before they could be harvested and the fragrant oil extracted. After speaking with Wayan, he hoped the Kuzma's desire to free themselves from working for the government and live in anonymity would lead them to manage the farm. Belevich, because of his skills, would have no trouble getting certified for floatplanes and seaplanes and finding employment transporting people in a nation with over eighteen thousand islands.

As predicted, immigration arrested Wayan, Eka, and Persik when the airport's facial recognition system displayed different names than those on their passports. Each was brought to separate rooms in the detention area and interrogated, immigration officials reticent to believe they worked for the government in a capacity that required them to have forged passports. Instead, they thought they'd apprehended three terrorists trying to infiltrate the country. Because of this, they weren't allowed to make a phone call, the authorities believing they'd tell other terrorists of their capture, enabling them to hide. Further adding to the official's disbelief of their story was their prisoner's steadfast refusal to say what they did for the government.

As a different officer did each interrogation, after they finished getting all they could, they left the suspected terrorists handcuffed to the table in the center of the room and went into the hall to compare notes.

"They're repeatedly telling the same story without deviation. That means they're well-versed in undergoing interrogation," one officer said.

"Why use a forged passport when each has a valid one and no outstanding warrants?"

"I asked," one official said, "but he refused to answer."

The other two immigration officers said the same.

"Let's put them in a cell and give them time to contemplate cooperating with us or living decades in a cage."

The other two officials agreed. But, as they headed back to the interrogation rooms, one official received a call from the bureaucrat three pay grades above his boss. "I received a call from the Minister of Defense," the bureaucrat began, "ordering me to release the three you took into custody. Return their belongings and escort them to the main terminal entrance, where a government vehicle will pick them up.

The official was stunned. "Should I forward their paperwork to you?"

"There will be no paperwork. Every scrap of paper the three of you created is to go into a shredder immediately. After that, ensure the videos of their arrests, questioning, and escort to their transport are erased."

"Seeing the surprised expression on the face of the person who took the call, the other officials asked what was going on.

"They were telling the truth."

Twenty minutes after that conversation, the three stepped into a government SUV and were taken to the top floor of the Jenderal Soedirman building—the Ministry of Defense headquarters. Ushered past security, through an empty waiting room, and past the empty desks of administrative assistants, they entered the office of a stout person in his mid-fifties who was five feet eight inches in height with hickory-colored skin and short salt and pepper hair. Defense Minister David Sondoro was sitting at the head of a conference table and, with a placid look, pointed them to the row of empty chairs. It was one-thirty in the morning.

Once they were seated, he opened the folder in front of him. "You three have had a busy ten days. You drained the accounts of two embassies," he said, sliding a printed spreadsheet toward Wayan, "got your Oymyakon tour group arrested and interrogated by the FSB before they were expelled from the country, had voice and data communication links to our Moscow embassy electronically jammed, had our Moscow dacha searched by the FSB, had your faces and passport aliases entered into Finnish databases with the notation that you're criminals who illegally fled across their border from Russia, and I'm sure committed numerous other crimes that have yet to come to my attention. Yet, somehow, while creating this chaos, you rescued the Kuzmas."

The three, sitting in a row to the Minister's right, looked as surprised as if someone had slapped them in the face.

"The Kuzmas, sir?" Wayan asked.

"We have an excellent facial recognition system. I put them into it in the event you were successful and returned here without time to give me advance notice. It was important they not be stopped at customs and immigration and draw undue attention to themselves by being detained. Their face was their ticket into Indonesia, not the name on their passport. The notation on the customs and immigration computer was that they let them enter the country without regard to the name on their passport and call me, no matter the time."

"And Belevich?" Wayan asked.

"You mean the Serbian. I didn't know his real name. We took him into custody along with the Kuzmas."

"Why are they in custody, and where are they? And why were we detained?"

"To answer your questions, all three are under guard in a conference room on the floor below. The Kuzmas are in custody because they're an important asset that needs protection. That should be obvious. The Serbian is in custody because I want to know more about his connection to them and if he has anything of intelligence value to share."

Wayan was about to weigh in with his thoughts when Sondoro cut him off and continued speaking.

"Now, tell me what happened from the time you landed in Moscow until you landed here, ending with an explanation of why you wanted to let the Kuzmas go," Sondoro said, pressing the red button on a digital recorder and sliding it toward the three.

Wayan, crestfallen knowing the Kuzmas wouldn't fulfill their dream of a life of anonymity in Sumbawa, reached for the coffee dispenser and poured himself a mug before responding. Persik and Eka followed, with Sondoro the last to refill.

For the next two hours, Wayan detailed what occurred, with Eka and Persik occasionally adding detail. Sondoro, not wanting to derail their train of thought, didn't interrupt except to order a second dispenser of coffee.

"I would have never guessed that Olena Kuzma was the genius behind the software that enabled her husband's camouflage technology. And she brought the software with her?"

"On a flash drive," Wayan confirmed.

"Remarkable. When you and your team left for Moscow, I confess I had my doubts that you'd return with the Kuzmas."

"That was clear when you told us we're nobodies, expendable, on our own, and if something goes wrong, there would be nothing linking our actions to a government-sanctioned operation. After all, with our pedigrees, who would hire us?"

"I apologize for that statement and for underestimating your skills. Even though detective Persik told me you have the unique ability to accomplish the impossible, I believed he was exaggerating. I didn't give you or Eka the benefit of the doubt or have the confidence in his judgment that I should. What will the two of you be working on next?"

"We have nothing pending."

"You have no clients?"

"It's been our unintentional business model."

"Getting back to the Kuzmas, in summarizing what happened, you said you felt there was no difference in them working for us or the Russians because we'd both keep them in protective custody, under constant surveillance, and forbid travel beyond our borders. The phrase you used was a gilded cage."

"I believe that's a statement of fact rather than a feeling."

"Because he's considered the father of camouflage technology, many governments want him to develop or enhance their program, voluntarily or not. That's a fact of life. He asked us to rescue him from the Russians."

"Rescue, not enslave. We took him from one gilded cage and put him in another," Wayan persisted.

The look on Sondoro's face showed he understood the argument but didn't want to concede the point. He changed the subject. "Any idea of what I should do with this pilot?" he asked, referring to Belevich.

"He knows nothing about the Kuzmas or their technology. He's a smuggler and opportunist who, as strange as it sounds, is trustworthy. If it weren't for him, we'd be in a Moscow jail, and the Kuzmas moved to a military base."

"He knows what this government did to get the doctor and his wife out of the Russian Federation, and the bribes to make that happen."

"He's a wanted man in Russia. If he returns, the FSB will interrogate him and put a bullet in his head."

"We paid for his retirement. He doesn't need to work another day and can hide quite well on what we wired to his offshore bank. However, as you said, if the FSB gets ahold of him, he'll be interrogated. What they discover will be a propaganda bonanza for the Russians, who'll spin it in a way that makes them look good while shattering our relationship with Finland. Therefore, I'm giving him the same protective umbrella we're providing the Kuzmas."

"Making him a virtual prisoner to keep your secret."

"There's no other way. As I told you at the start, I intend to barter this cutting-edge technology with other governments, particularly the United States. I'm sorry I can't give the Kuzmas or Belevich the freedom to go anywhere or do whatever they want, but that's the hand they've been dealt in life."

Wayan, whose face was red with anger, was about to tell Sondoro what he thought of his last statement when Eka interrupted.

"Do you mind if we speak with them before we leave?" she asked.

Sondoro thought for a moment, then granted their request knowing neither the Kuzmas nor Belevich could escape.

"Where are they going?" Persik asked.

"Someplace that's extremely secure because few besides senior Ministry officials know of its existence," Sondoro answered, implying that he, Wayan, and Eka wouldn't be one of the few.

They took the elevator to the floor below, the two uniformed soldiers with automatic weapons in front of them backing away upon seeing Sondoro. Continuing down the hall to the conference room, two similarly dressed and armed soldiers stepped aside from the door as Wayan, Eka, and Persik followed the Minister inside.

The conference room was large, dominated by an enormous rectangular table in the center, with eight chairs to a side and one at either end. Food and refreshments were on the table.

The meeting was short, ending with the Kuzmas thanking Wayan, Eka, and Persik again for getting them out of Russia.

"I hope we'll meet again someday," Wayan said, shaking Fedir's hand and pressing the pin he'd stealthily taken off his jacket lapel into his palm.

Forty-five minutes after Colonel Stasik Nazarov enlisted the help of the FSBs technology geeks, they found six individuals—three from India, two from Estonia, and one from Serbia, who purchased last-minute tickets from Tallinn to Jakarta. That the Estonian capital was a short ferry ride across the Gulf of Finland from Helsinki, and that the four were not traveling from their native countries, made the FSB colonel suspicious.

Because Estonia was formerly part of the Soviet Union before declaring independence, and Serbia was part of Yugoslavia, a former communist state, the FSB had historical access to those government networks, the intrusion becoming stealthier with technological advances. Therefore, it only took minutes for the geeks to confirm that the Estonian and Indian passports were forged because both were numbered sequentially, the odds of that occurring being higher than winning a lottery. This led Nazarov to believe that the forger had obtained authentic blank passports, most likely from corrupt embassy officials, and added the photograph, date of birth, and relevant information.

The routing showed the six fugitives would take a day and a half to reach Jakarta. In contrast, if he flew from Moscow to the Indonesian capital on Qatar Airways, he and the six soldiers accompanying him would arrive in half the time, getting their visas upon landing.

Lazarev made it clear before he left that his mission would be a success if he kidnapped the Kuzmas and got them out of Indonesia before the government could mount an organized search effort. In trying to figure out how to make that happen, the colonel thought back a decade ago to an FSB operation in Mexico City where an undercover agent was rescued from a heavy police guard and returned to Moscow. He reasoned that, with minor modifications, the same operation would be effective in kidnapping the Kuzmas.

The Qatar Airways flight was on time, and Nazarov and the six thugs accompanying him got their entry visas at the Jakarta Airport at eight-thirty in the morning. After clearing customs and immigration, they were met by the embassy's FSB agent in charge. The colonel and his men got into the two vans and were taken to a local restaurant, where he was handed the keys to the vehicles.

"Everything you requested is in the back of the vans. Their flight from Singapore is on time, and they'll arrive at terminal three at midnight," the agent said.

"When will your men be in position?" the colonel asked.

"At ten this evening."

"And the charter?"

"Also ready at ten at the general aviation terminal on the opposite side of the airport. The perimeter road will take you there."

"I'll make a dry run before then. What about customs and immigration at that terminal?"

"There's only one officer on duty at night. Since all of you have valid passports and visas and entered the country legally, there won't be an issue."

"To be clear, everyone dies but the older couple, who I'll identify. Their safety is paramount. After we leave, you'll take the bodies to the embassy and dispose of them in the usual manner," the colonel said, referring to placing them in the basement furnace used to dispose of classified materials.

Nazarov was the first to see the Kuzmas, along with the person he deduced was the Serbian because he didn't appear to be from India, being escorted from terminal number three and surrounded by four security guards as they walked to a waiting military police SUV. Once inside, it took off like a bat out of hell with lights flashing. The two vans followed but couldn't get close on the winding streets before the SUV arrived at the Ministry of Defense headquarters, where it pulled into a side alley. The roll-up door at the end raised, and the vehicle descended into the underground parking garage.

The colonel was in a quandary, not knowing how long the Kuzmas would be inside the building or the location of the other fugitives. If the couple didn't leave until daylight, when traffic in Jakarta became horrific, he'd have no chance of implementing the Mexico City plan and apprehending them. He could only stay outside the building, hoping they'd be moved while it was still dark. He directed the vans to park across the street from the garage entrance and wait.

While Nazarov was waiting, a second SUV arrived, and through the non-tinted windows, he saw Wayan inside. As with the other vehicle, it went down the side alley and entered the underground garage.

Two hours and fifteen minutes after the Kuzmas' SUV arrived at the Jenderal Soedirman building, the colonel saw the roll-up door raise and an SUV poised to exit. Making a leap of faith that the couple was inside, he said: "do it," to the person in the backseat, who had a computer on his lap.

Typing quickly on his keyboard, the tech, one of two he brought from Moscow, began linking with the vehicle's controller area network bus, or CAN bus, which allowed the car's microcontrollers and other devices to communicate with each other's applications without a host computer.

"Got you," the tech said. An instant later, as the SUV pulled into the street and turned left, its engine quit.

Immediately afterward, four of Nazarov's men ran to it and, using a window punch, smashed through the front and rear windows and tased the guards. The Kuzmas, confused by what was happening, were dragged to a van and shoved inside.

As the Kuzmas vehicle was being attacked, Wayan, Eka, Persik, and Belevich were in the parking garage waiting for their driver to take them to the airport for their departure to Bali; Belevich accompanying them because he was going to the same airport for a flight that would take him to his gilded cage.

Because of the second SUVs imminent departure, and the impending arrival of the driver, the roll-up door remained open after the Kuzmas departure. With the lack of gunfire or shouting outside, the four fugitives' first sign that something had happened was when one of the tased guards had recovered enough to stumble down the ramp and yell that the Kuzmas had been taken. The four reacted immediately. Wayan got into the driver's seat of the government SUV, with Eka beside him and Persik and Belevich in the back, the vehicle laying rubber as it raced out of the garage.

15

"Which way did they go?" Wayan asked Eka, who already had the cell phone out of her pocket and was accessing the app that allowed her to track the pin that Wayan gave Fedir.

"Turn left," she screamed.

Wayan barely had time to turn, narrowly missing the vehicles parked on the other side of the street.

She directed him through the city for the next five minutes before determining that the vans were headed for the main highway.

"How far are we behind them?" Wayan asked.

"Two miles," she answered after checking the app.

"Let me see if I can shave off some time by taking a shortcut that the locals use to get to the highway," Wayan said as he began weaving through side streets. The former detective had spent several months in Jakarta while on a case and was introduced to these shortcuts by members of the local police force.

The SUV was built for comfort and wasn't meant to be driven as a sports car, which was how Wayan was driving it. The suspension on a sports car was stiff, which provided better handling. In contrast, the SUVs suspension was soft, meaning it tended to roll when it rounded corners at excessive speeds, increasing the risk of losing control and crashing if the tires lost contact with the ground. Although Wayan's shortcut involved a labyrinth-like course, he maintained an aggressive rate of speed to try and lessen the two miles between the SUV and the vans. The result was that the vehicle skidded into every turn and nearly flipped over several times as it wove through the city on its way to the highway.

The navigation system in Nazarov's vehicle showed the airport was five miles ahead. The Kuzma had been sedated and put in the diplomatic containers in the back of his van; each affixed with a diplomatic seal. The sedation would last two hours, enough time for the containers to be loaded onto the aircraft and cleared by customs, who were prohibited from looking inside. Once airborne, he'd take the couple from the containers and have his men watch them for the rest of the flight.

With the airport in sight, the driver of Nazarov's van noticed a set of headlights in his rearview mirror rapidly closing on the vans, even though he was going seventy-five mph, the max he could get out of the aging vehicle. He alerted the colonel.

"I don't know who that could be, but I'm not taking any chances," Nazarov said. "Contact the other van and have them take out the vehicle behind them," he told the tech in the back, who was sitting on the floor.

The driver who received the order from Nazarov's van relayed it to the others, after which they rolled down their windows, extended their automatic weapons, and opened fire on the closing vehicle. However, unlike in the movies, gauging the distance and elevation of a car on an unlit highway at night is difficult. Therefore, despite their best efforts, none of their rounds stopped the vehicle, and it continued to close on them.

Agreeing that sticking their guns out the window of a shaking vehicle wouldn't provide the stability they needed to hit the car, the two men decided to get in the back of the van where they could better stabilize their aim. However, unlike the lead van, which had the rear benches removed so the containers could fit, this one still had them. Therefore, it took a few moments to climb over the seats and sit cross-legged on the deck with their elbows on their knees, a position that would provide the stability needed to destroy the vehicle following them.

After getting into position, one of the men unfastened the latch, and both kicked the rear doors open. Their eyes widened in disbelief when they saw the SUV was feet away and closing fast. In a sitting position, neither had time to grab ahold of anything before the impact and were jolted backward when the SUV struck the left side of the van and continued speeding up. The impact caused the van's rear tires to lose traction, skid to the left, and flip over several times before sliding to a stop.

Wayan and the three fugitives with him never saw this finale because, as the van skidded, he adjusted the direction of his vehicle to the right and continued chasing the lead van. This technique, which he learned on the force, was called the PIT maneuver, the initials standing for precision immobilization technique, which turned the fleeing vehicle sideways, causing the driver to lose control or stop.

"Nicely done," Persik said. "It's a good thing Eka was right about the signal coming from the first vehicle."

"The signal's still in front of us," she said, showing her cell phone to Persik so he could see the blue dot on her screen.

"Any idea how we stop that van before it gets to the airport without killing the Kuzmas?"

"We'll play that one by ear because it looks like we're going to get there about the same time," Wayan said, following the van down on the highway offramp and seeing the lights from the general aviation terminal a mile ahead.

As they got closer, the cargo plane parked behind the terminal came into view, its large loading hatch, which was five feet behind the cockpit, open. A portable stairway was on the left side of the hatch, the space to the right enough for the forklift to place the containers onboard. One of the flight crew stood beside the ramp, with a uniformed customs and immigration official next to him. Both vehicles screeched to a halt in front of the aircraft at the same time.

Wayan, Eka, Persik, and Belevich ran from the SUV. As they approached the vehicle, they stopped in surprise upon seeing Nazarov, who got out of the van and calmly handed the customs and immigration officer the forms to transport the diplomatic containers.

The inspector looked at the forms, saw they were correctly filled out, and told the forklift operator he could put the diplomatic containers onto the aircraft, after which one of Nazarov's men opened the rear of the van.

"Wait. This person kidnapped two people from the Ministry of Defense, and they're in those containers," Wayan said to the inspector as the first was lifted out of the van.

"They'll say anything to look inside," Nazarov responded. "These containers are the property of the Russian Federation and cannot be opened except by an authorized embassy official."

"He's correct," the official responded, as the forklift placed the first container onboard and was returning for the second. "Are you accompanying the containers?" the official Nazarov.

"Three of us will be departing on this charter," he responded, handing the officer three passports. He'd let their embassy deal with the consequences of the crash and the three men in it.

The official took his time examining them and carefully stamped each before returning them to Nazarov. I have the diplomatic customs declaration for the containers, but not your customs and immigration departure forms," he said to the three men standing in front of him. They're a requirement for any non-citizen leaving the country. Please fill these out," he said, taking the forms from the clipboard in his hand and giving it to the three men. The forms, which were in Indonesian and English, took several minutes to complete, with the officer helping them where they had difficulty understanding the meaning.

"The three of you are free to board your charter and leave," the official said. "But I'll need their passports and customs declarations if they're to accompany you," he said, pointing to the Kuzmas, who were unsteadily descending the boarding ramp with Wayan who, while the Russians were focusing on getting their documentation straight with the customs and immigration officer, and with the pilot removing the chocks in front of the aircraft's wheels and conducting his pre-flight checks, went onto the aircraft and broke the diplomatic seals with the plane's fire ax. The co-pilot, who wore headphones and was speaking with the tower, didn't see or hear what was happening in the rear of the aircraft.

"Arrest them," Nazarov demanded as the three stepped onto the tarmac.

"They've broken no customs and immigration laws."

"He opened diplomatic containers."

"I didn't see that. They were sealed when they left Indonesian jurisdiction and placed onboard your charter. Are the two of you leaving on this plane?" the officer asked the Kuzmas, receiving a negative reply from the couple. "Then I wish the three of you a safe journey," the official said, pointing the colonel and his men to the boarding ramp.

Nazarov knew the three of them could overpower the officer. However, he wasn't sure he could get past Wayan, Persik, and Belevich. As bad as things were, assaulting an Indonesian government official would create a diplomatic stir and invite an investigation that the FSB wouldn't want to be publicized. Therefore, with great self-control, he and his men boarded the aircraft. Five minutes later, the cargo plane was airborne, the customs and immigration official and forklift operator having left as the plane taxied to the runway.

"This is only a reprieve," Persik said. "Sondoro is going to scour the city for the six of us, and with his resources, it won't take him long to find us."

"I know. We need to get the Kuzmas and Belevich to Sumbawa before he finds them," Wayan said.

"How do we do that?" Eka asked.

"Nabar," Wayan answered.

"We have a problem," Wayan said without preamble when Nabar answered the phone at his farm at four-forty in the morning, having just finished his workout which began each day at four. The special forces captain was bald, six feet one inch tall, with light brown skin, hazel eyes, and a thick muscular torso that gave the impression that punches would rebound off him.

"With the three I'm to pick up at the airport later this morning?"

"Yes."

"What kind of problem?"

"The type that means they have to come to Sumbawa by boat."

"Why?"

"Because Sondoro is after all of us," Wayan answered.

"Defense Minister Sondoro?" Nabar asked with astonishment.

"I'll explain everything when you get here."

"Where is here?"

"The general aviation terminal of the Jakarta airport," Wayan replied.

"There's a flight that leaves at five-thirty, which will get me to Jakarta in less than two hours."

"While you're at it, see if Tamala can come; we may need his contacts," Wayan said, referring to Major Langit Tamala, another Indonesia Army special forces group member. He and Nabar were stationed at Halim Air Base in East Jakarta, which was nineteen miles from the international airport. Nabar left there the day before to go to Sumbawa in anticipation of meeting the arriving trio.

"I'll ask."

At seven-thirty, two camouflaged Land Rover Defenders, one driven by Nabar and the other by Tamala, pulled in front of the general aviation terminal, a sign above the phone indicating that outside of the eight am to midnight working hours, fuel and other services would be provided by on-call airport staff. The six fugitives, sitting on the concrete floor with their back against the building, stood when the vehicles arrived. Tamala and two of his friends had driven three Defenders to the airport to meet Nabar, his friends returning to Halim in one while Tamala and Nabar took the remaining two to the general aviation terminal.

Nabar, who had a thing for Eka before she and Wayan became an item, smiled at her before he and Tamala exchanged introductions with the Kuzmas and Belevich.

"Let's go to a diner near here and get a cup of coffee and something to eat," Tamala said, looking at the tired faces staring at him.

"That's a good idea," Wayan responded, the weariness clear in his voice.

Tamala divided the group, taking Wayan, Eka, and Persik with him while the rest drove with Nabar. The diner, which was ten minutes away, had seven patrons when they arrived. Tamala and Nabar pulled two rectangular tables together so the eight could sit together. After coffee was poured and everyone ordered breakfast, Wayan summarized what happened and why Sondoro was anxious to find the Kuzmas.

"How can anyone who can only get one client at a time consistently get into so much trouble?" Tamala asked.

"You've had this type of trouble before?" Fedir inquired.

"It was different," Wayan said defensively.

"He's been chased by organ harvesters, the Italian Mafia, the local Mafia, kidnapped by North Korea, hunted by Russian and

North Korean generals, pursued by Iranians, and I almost forgot, had a boat blown out from beneath him and was rescued while floating on a piece of wreckage," Tamala volunteered.

"So, what we've been through, and the danger experienced with the Russians in pursuit of us, is nothing unusual?" Olena asked.

"Let's get back to how we can get you and your husband to Nabar's farm on Sumbawa," Wayan segued.

"Jakarta is on the island of Java," Nabar explained, looking at the Kuzmas and Belevich. "The only way to leave is by boat or plane. Sondoro knows that, and he'll have the airports and marinas covered. Therefore, getting off Java will be a challenge."

No one could argue with what Nabar said, the silence extending for over a minute as the food was brought to the table and the coffee mugs refilled.

"I have an idea," Belevich said.

"We could use one," Wayan replied.

"You told me that Sumbawa is approximately seven hundred fifty miles from here. I can fly us there."

"As Nabar said, every commercial and private airport in and around Jakarta will be monitored. Our escape will have embarrassed Sondoro, and he'll be pissed. He'll have the military stationed at every transport facility, be it marina or airfield, on the island," Wayan countered.

"I'm not talking about renting a plane. We're stealing one."

"You're not serious," Persik said, figuring out what Belevich wanted to do.

"Skiplane, seaplane, floatplane—they're all the same aircraft with a different undercarriage. Indonesian radar won't be any better than they have in Russia or Finland. If I stay low, we'll be undetectable."

"He has a point, and it doesn't seem like we have another option," Eka said, garnering agreement from the rest of the table.

"Assuming we get to Sumbawa, what will you do with the plane? It'll be reported as stolen, and Sondoro will know where you and the Kuzmas are when it's found," Wayan asked.

Belevich said what he intended to do.

That solves our problem, but what about the three of you?" Fedir asked, looking at Wayan, Eka, and Persik. "When the Minister can't find us, he'll arrest you for helping us escape."

"We'll figure something out," Wayan answered, his words unconvincing to himself and the others.

"Maybe I can help by giving you something to barter," Olena said, removing the flash drive from her belt buckle and sliding it to him. "This will let your country solve the motion limitations of active camouflage technology and put them years ahead of the Russians."

Wayan was speechless for a few seconds before picking up the drive. "You may need this for your bartering if Sondoro finds you."

"I'm counting on you to negotiate something that includes leaving us in peace."

"I'm not sure I know how to cast that large a shadow."

"You'll figure it out," Olena confidently replied.

16

The Ancol Marina was sixteen miles from the café and the closest place where seaplanes docked. Because of the number of islands that comprised Indonesia, seaplanes and floatplanes were familiar sights throughout the country, providing necessary transport to towns, villages, and cities which didn't have an airport nearby. Although the words seaplane and floatplane are often used interchangeably, these aircraft are different. The fuselage or belly of a floatplane does not contact the water because it rides on floats or pontoons. In contrast, a seaplane's fuselage rides on the water during takeoffs and landings. Belevich, knowing the difference, expressed his desire to steal a floatplane because it better matched the takeoff and landing characteristics of his former skiplane, where the fuselage was above the snow.

Although everyone got into the Defenders and went to the marina, only Belevich, Nabar, and the Kuzmas would go to Sumbawa. Tamala would return to base and cover for Nabar while Wayan, Eka, and Persik went to the office of an attorney who Eka knew to draw up a barter agreement with Sondoro before leaving the other Defender outside the base for Tamala to retrieve.

Knowing this was the last time they might see one another, and with all they'd been through and the bonding that occurred,

Olena couldn't hold it together and cried, embracing Eka, followed by Wayan and Persik. "Thank you doesn't begin to express our gratitude for what you've done and what might happen to you for helping us," she said to the three.

"We couldn't be happier that you're finally able to escape your gilded cage," Eka replied.

"I believe this belongs to you," Fedir said as he tried handing Wayan the tracking pin, only to have him push it away.

"Keep it. It'll let me know that you and Olena are safe," after which everyone exchanged a warm embrace.

The place for their farewell was chosen by Belevich who, as they drove through the marina, saw a Cessna 206 floatplane, which was forty-five inches shorter and with two fewer seats than his Cessna skiplane. It was still early, and those at the marina were at the opposite end where the boats were docked.

"This will be like flying my plane," Belevich said, as he walked down the ramp to the plane.

Although the aircraft's door was locked, Nabar quickly opened it using the tip of his knife. Belevich got into the pilot seat and, turning on the battery, saw that the fuel tanks were full. Having no idea how to get to Sumbawa, he was about to download the aeronautical charts for the area onto his cell phone when he decided to look in the back of the aircraft, knowing most pilots kept area charts in their plane. Therefore, he wasn't surprised when he saw a worn brown leather case containing a set of aeronautical flight charts.

"Untie us," Belevich said to Nabar, after which he told the Kuzmas to strap themselves into the two seats behind him.

As Nabar got into the co-pilot's seat, Belevich spent the next ten minutes studying the aeronautical charts and plotting a course for Sumbawa. He had no trouble starting the engine, as the controls were virtually a duplicate of his now demised skiplane. However, as soon as the engine was turning, even with the throttle at idle, the plane moved out of its slip and toward open water.

"You can't brake on the water," Belevich said to himself, realizing at idle he was still generating power and was sitting in a boat with wings. He next discovered that the foot pedals worked the same as those on land-based aircraft, although he didn't know that was because the floats had rudders and a keel running down the centerline, which allowed him to steer the plane in the water the same as he would on a hard surface runway.

After distancing himself from the marina, he looked at the windsock on shore and turned the aircraft into the wind. Pushing the throttle forward, the plane accelerated rapidly because the water was choppy, meaning the floats had less adhesion to it, although Belevich didn't know that's why the Cessna was airborne so quickly. As it lifted off, he turned to a south-easterly heading that would take him to the side of Sumbawa where Nabar said his farm was located. At the plane's top speed of one hundred seventy mph, and because of the wind, they'd land in a hair over four hours.

Following the escape of the six fugitives, Sondoro excoriated building security and asked for the camera feeds. These showed the Kuzmas being kidnapped by unknown assailants in two vans that had stolen license plates, and that one of his security vehicles gave chase. Later, he learned that Wayan and the other fugitives were in that SUV. The Jakarta surveillance system was able to follow the three vehicles for two blocks, after which they left the coverage area, one shortcoming of the system being that it was a point rather than a tracking system, meaning it looked at vehicles and persons at strategic spots and areas in the city, but couldn't track them throughout the city of eleven million because installing such coverage exceeded the money in government coffers. It wasn't until six am, two hours and fifteen minutes after the Kuzmas were kidnapped, that he learned a customs and immigration official had cleared three Russians to accompany two diplomatic containers aboard a charter aircraft to Moscow. The official noted in his report that one Russian became incensed when a middle-aged man and a woman stepped off the plane and refused to accompany him. From his description, Sondoro knew it was the Kuzmas. His report also noted that four others were at the general aviation terminal, their descriptions matching Wayan, Eka, Persik, and Belevich, and that they remained behind when the charter departed.

The Minister believed the six were still on the island of Java, given the time of day and that their names were still in the national database. If they bought a ticket or used their credit card, he'd be notified. He also ordered their photos be sent to every transportation hub and law enforcement agency, indicating they were only wanted for questioning.

The first indication that he was correct in assuming the fugitives were still in Java was later that morning when he received a call from an attorney who said that Gunter Wayan gave him a message to deliver.

"Your client is a criminal and a national security risk," Sondoro said. "Tell me where he and the others are, or I'll put you in the cell meant for them."

"Many of my clients are criminals. If they weren't, I'd be unemployed. To answer your question, I don't know where they are. If you want to hear what Wayan has to say, we can meet in thirty minutes. If not, I fulfilled my client's request by contacting you, and we can both go about our day. Oh, and if you ever threaten to put me in jail again for representing a client, I'll squeeze your balls so hard in our negotiations that you won't be able to breathe."

"What negotiations?"

"You'll see."

"Thirty minutes," Sondoro said and ended the call.

When the attorney entered his office, Sondoro motioned him to the conference table and took his usual seat at its head. The attorney then handed him a three-page agreement, the contents of which Wayan had dictated and which he put in legalese. The Minister read what he was given.

"What's on the flash drive?" Sondoro asked.

"My client told me to tell you it's Olena Kuzma's software and Fedir Kuzma's hardware designs."

"Do you mind if I call someone to take a look?"

"I expected you would. You'll need this one-time code," he said, handing him a slip of paper containing seven upper and lower case letters and an equal number of symbols. "A second access code is needed to transfer the data. Three failed attempts erase the drive."

Sondoro called his lead camouflage technology scientist to his office. Since it was nine-thirty in the morning, the tech was in his lab, which was fifteen minutes from the Ministry.

When the scientist arrived, Sondoro explained what he wanted and handed him the flash drive. Forty minutes later, the scientist finished his review and told the Minister that what he'd seen was genius and that it would take a while to understand the groundbreaking hardware, and the software algorithms that interacted with it.

Once the scientist left, Sondoro swiveled his chair slightly to the right to face the attorney better. "Let me summarize your client's demands outlined in the agreement you presented," Sondoro said, "to ensure there are no misunderstandings."

"That makes sense."

"Fedir and Olena Kuzma and Kirill Belevich, known by those names and any alias they may have used, are pardoned for all crimes, which will be expunged from our government databases."

"Government and local databases," the attorney corrected.

"And local databases," Sondoro stated. "They're to be granted Indonesian citizenship and issued passports, which are renewable for the rest of their lives. They are allowed to live anonymously without local or government surveillance or contact. However, if their location is discovered," Sondoro read after picking up the agreement, "such location will not be shared with another government and will be protected within national databases with the highest security classification with compartmentalized viewing on a need-to-know basis."

"Do you think I'd let a foreign government kidnap them if I knew their location? That's what this demand is about, isn't it?"

"You may if it were the United States, Great Britain, France, and so forth, and you got a substantive arms or technology package in return," the attorney said, staring Sondoro in the eyes.

The Minister broke off eye contact and continued summarizing what he'd read. "Gunter Wayan, Eka Endah, and Suton Persik also want the same pardon and expungement, prohibition from being surveilled by the local and national government, guaranteed renewal of their passports, an agreement of no-reprisal against their family, friends, or acquaintances, and a letter of commendation for their services. They also want three wires for services in the amounts you requested, and your fee paid by the Ministry."

"The amounts I specified," the attorney corrected.

"Don't you think receiving payment for a service agreement they breached is dishonest?"

"Dishonesty should come naturally to you, minister. This is the fee you agreed to pay Wayan and anyone who accompanied him. Do you really have a problem with the amount considering the value of the flash drive?"

Sondoro knew the payment for services was minuscule considering the value of the drive and let the comment on his character slide rather than get into it with a person over whom he had very little leverage. He continued. "A new Cessna 206 floatplane is to be delivered to the Ancol marina and given to the person who reported a similar aircraft stolen. There are other demands, all of which I can live with."

"If you adhere to this agreement, our copy of the flash drive I handed you will never find the light of day. You'll never have to see or hear from my clients again."

Sondoro got up, walked to the credenza behind the conference table, and poured two mugs of coffee, handing one to the attorney. "There's a misunderstanding," Sondoro said, retaking his seat. "I may want to engage your clients in the future if they agree to abide by the terms of their service agreement and not change it."

"I don't understand why you want anything further to do with them."

"Although I'm unhappy with not having the Kuzmas work for me, I believe your clients accomplished the impossible. The teamwork and resourcefulness they displayed can't be taught. It either exists, or it doesn't. If my back is to the wall and internal resources fall short, I'd have no hesitation in hiring them."

"Because they're nobodies?"

"It was a stupid statement that implies they're dispensable and of no importance. I hope this will amend that mistake," he said, removing a pen from his pocket and signing and dating the agreement presented by the attorney.

Belevich landed the floatplane off the coast of Sumbawa at eleven in the morning. The landing wasn't the smoothest, but after a couple of bounces, the Cessna 206 stopped three hundred and fifty yards from where it first touched down, a short distance from shore. The Russian/Serbian taxied the aircraft to an empty commercial dock, let his passengers off, and then taxied to the blue water offshore, which was several hundred feet deep.

Each aircraft float had four watertight compartments, preventing it from flooding and sinking. Belevich didn't know this safety feature when he took the fire ax from the plane's rear and chopped one hole in each float below the waterline. When the aircraft remained stable above the water, he took a more drastic approach and indiscriminately began chopping additional holes along the waterline. Finally, the aircraft started to sink. As the plane was submerging, he removed his shoes, dove into the ocean, and going with the current, swan the thousand yards to shore in around thirty minutes. Nabar was there when he stepped out of the water.

Twenty minutes after the floatplane sank, a worker from Nabar's sandalwood farm arrived and drove the four to the farm, which was forty minutes away.

Wayan, Eka, and Persik picked up their boarding passes at the Guarda Airlines ticket counter and passed through security without issue, their plane landing at Bali's Denpasar International Airport thirty minutes after Nabar and his new tenants arrived at the farm.

All three turned on their cell phones when they deplaned, Wayan telling Eka and Persik that he received a text from Nabar that everyone was safe at his farm. Another text was from the attorney, indicating that Sondoro wired the consulting fee into their three bank accounts.

"This was your consulting gig. I have a job, or may still have a job," Persik corrected.

"The money is already in your account," Wayan said.

"I don't feel right about taking it. The police association's benevolent fund could use it more than me."

"I can't think of a better use for the money. We'll do the same," Wayan said, Eka nodding in agreement.

"Getting paid by clients is how you earn a living," Persik countered.

"As the maximum number of clients that I've had at one time has never exceeded one, I'm used to being poor. Therefore, in all fairness, it's not much of a sacrifice," Wayan countered, drawing laughs from Persik and Eka.

As they exited the terminal and stopped in front of the taxi stand, each knew that after an intense ten days in which they were inseparable, they were about to go their separate ways. Wayan and Eka were headed to their home at the Bulgari Resort in Uluwatu, eleven miles from the airport. Persik's residence was four miles away in South Kuta. His house was on a remote stretch of beach with few tourists because it wasn't near a major resort like the Bulgari. Persik, who looked particularly downtrodden, was given a hug and kiss on the cheek by Eka.

"Coffee tomorrow morning on the patio?" she asked, drawing a smile from the detective and a look of consternation from Wayan, who remembered that's exactly how they got talked into rescuing the Kuzmas.

"I'll be there," he responded before getting into a taxi.

"That was nice of you," Wayan said in a voice that implied his statement had another meaning.

"You know he was going to drop by anyway."

"Yeah, but I can always hope," he replied, his comment earning an elbow in the ribs.

17

Three weeks after Nazarov returned to his office in Yakutsk, the Finnish Minister of Foreign Affairs summoned the Russian ambassador to Finland and gave him a verbal shellacking. Reading from a report, he cited a series of sovereignty violations that included a Russian military aircraft crossing the border into his country and an FSB officer chasing a suspect throughout it without permission. He also said this officer ordered the police to arrest one of its citizens without proof of wrongdoing. The ambassador, caught by surprise, said he'd immediately call for an investigation.

"Don't take long," the Minister cautioned, "or our Ambassador to the United Nations will read this report to the Security Council, which guarantees your violations of our sovereignty will receive global attention."

"Is that a threat?"

"It's a statement of fact."

By happenstance, later that same day, Indonesia's Ministry of Foreign Affairs summoned the Russian ambassador to his office and demanded an explanation of why a Russian colonel and the five who accompanied him from Moscow kidnapped two Indonesian citizens as they left the Ministry of Defense and assaulted its security staff. He also demanded to know why this colonel attempted to hide them in a diplomatic container onboard an aircraft chartered to fly to Moscow. The ambassador, knew nothing of the incident and offered to forward the matter for investigation.

"You have a week, Dmitri. After that, I'm recommending the Defense Minister cancel our order for your Su-35 aircraft and replace them with America's F-35."

The ambassador, who knew that order was worth billions, even without the associated spare parts and training, informed Moscow.

When these complaints were brought to the attention of the President of the Russian Federation and the Minister of Foreign Affairs, and knowing the name of the officer responsible for the violations of sovereignty, Lazarev was summoned to the Kremlin and eviscerated by the president for his recklessness which, in Kremlin parlance, meant getting caught. After explaining what occurred, the Minister said a quiet diplomatic solution was in everyone's interest. The president agreed. Taking the initiative, the Minister of Foreign Affairs phoned his Finnish counterpart and proposed that he forget about the rogue actions of a Russian officer. In return for this amnesia, his government would return to Finland the two hundred sixty million euros it recently paid for importing goods from Finland. The Finnish Minister agreed.

Resolving the situation with Indonesia was more complex because their agents abducted the Kuzmas from Russian soil, the same infringement of sovereignty they were accused of committing. The only difference between the violations was that Russian agents were caught, and the Indonesians weren't. They also didn't believe they could accuse the Indonesians of violating their sovereignty without it coming to light that they kidnapped the Kuzmas from Ukraine and killed security guards.

"What do they want to maintain their silence and forget this happened?" the president asked his Minister of Foreign Affairs.

"They didn't say."

"What do you suggest?"

The Minister thought for a while before responding. "That we both forget about each other's transgressions because I don't believe their Minister of Foreign Affairs knew his country had agents on our soil doing the same thing he's accusing us of."

That worked; the ministers spoke to each other, agreeing each nation would suffer diplomatically if these transgressions were exposed.

Lazarev ground his teeth and kept silent during these discussions. He felt strongly that the Russian Federation shouldn't try to placate countries. Instead, it said what it was going to do, and they fell in line, or else. What the president and Minister needed was to take a Stalinesque approach, returning to the philosophy of the Soviet Union and stop being so conciliatory. However, although he wanted to offer these suggestions, they would go counter to what the most powerful person in the Kremlin wanted. Knowing that he was on thin ice and was there to answer questions, he remained silent. Later that afternoon, returning to his office, he manifested his frustration by making two personnel changes.

The weather in Oymyakon had deteriorated rapidly since the fugitives bolted from the settlement in the stolen bus, an arctic blast bringing the temperature to minus sixty-two degrees Fahrenheit at night, rising to minus fifty-six during the day. The FSB officer tasked with watching Olena Kuzma was transferred to Ust Nera. Although the temperature was minus forty-nine degrees, nearly as crisp as in Oymyakon, the population was ten times larger. He especially liked that it had a train station, airport, restaurants, bars, and the other trappings of civilization previously unavailable to him. Because he was demoted two ranks for letting the detainee escape, the last thing he expected was to leave Oymyakon. His replacement, with whom he was switching duty stations, was Major Stasik Nazarov, who had recently been demoted two ranks for screwing something up, or so he heard.

On the second day at his duty station, Nazarov, who was used to the cold but not the area around Oymyakon, got lost when going for a walk and froze to death. His body was found the following day by an FSB agent sent to bring him supplies, who miraculously stumbled on his body. That no one went for a walk when the temperature hovered around minus sixty, and that the major's parka was missing, was deemed odd but not questioned.

Lazarev was a thornier problem for the Kremin. The four-star couldn't be demoted and told to retire because of the publicity it would generate. Therefore, another solution was found, and the same day Nazarov met his end, the director of the FSB suffered a heart attack while at his desk. The president declared an autopsy unnecessary, eliminating the possibility that the poison placed in his tea by someone in the kitchen would be detected. The president felt that Lazarev's aide, who knew an uncomfortable amount of information about what happened, couldn't die, or it would create doubt that his boss succumbed to a heart attack. Therefore, he was sent to Oymyakon to replace the recently deceased major and advised that any recall of what transpired with the Kuzmas would result in his being replaced. He got the point.

Although Nabar wasn't a farmer and knew little about growing sandalwood trees, worth twenty thousand dollars each, his neighbors did. They agreed to teach the Kuzmas how to grow and maintain them. The couple took to their new profession with vigor, working from dawn to dusk to implement what they'd been taught. Three months after they arrived, they felt comfortable enough to tell Nabar they could manage the farm.

Today started as usual: the Ukrainian couple got up just before daylight, which was five fifty-three am, and began their chores after a quick bite. At ten am, their routine was interrupted by the sound of a vehicle coming down the road. Going to investigate, they saw Nabar driving a car with Wayan in the front and Eka and Persik in the rear.

Eka laughed when she saw the Kuzmas wearing a seraung, a conical-shaped sunhat made from palm leaves, and the same work clothes and boots worn by the other laborers. After exchanging hugs and greetings, they went inside the house where, sipping teh manis, or sweet tea, the Kuzmas described their love of farming.

"Is this a social visit, or is there more?" Olena asked.

"Both," Wayan answered, updating them on Nazarov's death, which was passed onto him by the Ministry of Defense.

"I admit that's a relief," Fedir said. "But I'm still unsure about the Minister's commitment to leaving us alone, even with the signed agreement."

"I believe that as they continue to develop your technology and it evolves, your usefulness will dissipate," Wayan said. "The last time we spoke, he said that his scientists were making discoveries that would improve your hardware design because of what was on the flash drive."

The Kuzmas visibly relaxed upon hearing that.

"Where's Belevich?" Eka asked.

"He's working for a floatplane operator," Fedir answered.

"Did he get certified?"

"No."

"Didn't the floatplane company ask for his license?"

"No. They took him up for a test flight and found, in his words, that he was an instinctive pilot."

"Meaning that he could take tourists and passengers between the islands?" Persik asked.

"That he was good at flying below radar."

"He's back to transporting illicit goods?" Wayan asked. "How could he find a smuggling network so fast?"

"He said he went to several floatplane charter companies, and all but one asked for his license. The other wanted to see his low-level flying skills. Belevich said he guessed what that was about and, after a frank conversation in which he chronicled some of his smuggling exploits, they put him to work."

Persik shook his head, wishing he hadn't heard what Fedir said, but had no intention of doing anything about it.

"He's only landed a floatplane once," Eka commented.

"He said the owner of the company gave him a few hours of instruction, enough to get him in the air and land."

Everyone laughed, knowing that Belevich was enjoying his illegal occupation.

They spent the next hour talking, laughing, and vowing to spend a weekend together in the future. When it was time to leave, the Kuzmas walked the four to their vehicle. Wayan, Eka, and Persik were flying to Bali, while Nabar was returning to his base in Jakarta.

Eka and Wayan were sitting on their patio the morning after returning from Sumbawa. It was six thirty-five, and they had a mug of coffee in their hands as they watched the magnificent sunrise at the edge of the Indian ocean. That calm was broken by the doorbell beside the gate, which led into their compound.

"Persik," Eka said, drawing a nod from Wayan, who got up and, pressing the gate and front door releases from a kitchen panel, began making the detective a Nespresso Intenso coffee.

"Good morning," Wayan said, handing him a mug and leading the way onto the patio, where Eka greeted the detective, receiving a kiss on both cheeks in return.

Persik, who was single and had no social life, made a habit of coming to their home unannounced, knowing that the couple spent their mornings on the patio. After spending an hour or two with them, he'd go to the office, sometimes returning to their home in the evening. Wayan and Eka considered him a family member and enjoyed being around the affable detective.

The detective's routine seldom varied. After finishing his first cup of coffee, he'd raid the refrigerator for breakfast, usually taking the salmon and putting a slice or two on a toasted bagel with slivers of onion and tomato. Wayan normally had the same, with Eka preferring a fruit plate. In the evening, Persik would cook dinner, picking up whatever they were having on his way. Although they would never admit it to him, they looked forward to his presence.

As he sipped his coffee, Eka asked if he would join them for dinner.

"That's tempting, but I have something going on tonight."

"A date?"

"I'll be supervising a night surveillance detail."

"A first lieutenant on surveillance?" Wayan questioned.

"I'm replacing a friend who's sick. Because the individuals surveilled may be terrorists, an onsite senior supervisor is required."

"Aren't terrorists the responsibility of Detachment eighty-eight?" Wayan asked, referring to the Indonesian National Police counter-terrorism force formed in response to the 2002 bombings in Bali.

"Not until we confirm they're terrorists and not hoods looking for a score," Persik answered.

Persik finished his coffee and went into the kitchen to fix breakfast, followed by Wayan.

Once he left, Wayan and Eka got dressed and spent the rest of the day organizing their records and files, something they kept putting off, and getting Eka's Range Rover serviced. Wayan's vehicle, a faded green 2000 Mahindra Jeep on life support was beyond help, and was used as their vehicle of last resort. They finished around five that evening and, after a light dinner and watching the sunset at six-fifteen, went to the resort's bar before returning at eight-thirty and retiring for the evening. Even though it was early, both had a habit of getting up in the middle of the night and going outside to experience the cool ocean air and smell of the sea, often reading before returning to bed when they started to doze off.

This evening started like every other, with Wayan and Eka in bed by eight-fifteen and on the patio a little past midnight. He fixed them a cup of chamomile tea because it didn't have caffeine, and brought the mugs onto the deck. After a few moments of silence, Wayan turned and faced Eka.

"Do you remember when I said I was extremely fond of you and that our friendship could develop into something more?"

"That was a year and a half ago. Do you remember what I said when you asked why I wanted to be with someone even though, as you said, I'd been offered significantly higher-paying jobs?"

"You said I was someone who helps those who can't help themselves, regardless of whether there's a payday at the end, and that being a part of that brought you great satisfaction. You also told me not to change."

"What did I do next?"

"Anna interrupted us," Wayan said, referring to Anna Bello, the resort's owner.

"Before that."

When Wayan didn't respond, Eka got up, bent down, placed a hand on either side of his face, and gave him a soft kiss on the lips that lingered before she gently broke it off.

"I still can't remember. Can you do that again?"

She did.

"You said you kissed me because you wanted to eliminate any barrier between us so that I wouldn't feel awkward having an intimate conversation or getting closer to you in the future."

"I also said that if I didn't kiss you, I might have gray hair by the time you got around to it."

"That's probably true."

"Why are you bringing this up?" she asked.

"Because I want you to know I've grown deeply in love with you. It's something I should have said long before now, but there's not a day that goes by that I don't realize having you in my life is the best thing that ever happened to me."

"I love you too, Wayan."

"Hoping that your bout of insanity continues, will you marry me?" he asked as he got down on one knee, took a ring from the pocket of his robe, and slid it onto her finger.

"With all my heart," she responded."

AUTHOR'S NOTES

This is a work of fiction, and the characters within are not meant to depict nor implicate anyone in the actual world. Moreover, representations of corruption, illegal activities, and actions taken by government and industry officials were done for the sake of the storyline. They don't represent or imply any illegality or nefarious activity by those who occupy or have occupied positions within government or industry. Substantial portions of *The Defector,* as stated below, are factual.

One of the most challenging aspects of writing this manuscript was keeping the times straight and in sync because of the numerous time zones in the storyline. One hundred forty-nine times had to be synchronized in this ten-day adventure, and they play an integral role in how the action unfolds. For example, while part of the action takes place in Oymyakon, another occurs in Ust Nera, a related series of events takes place in Moscow, and so forth. Additionally, to make these interactions as realistic as possible, I used actual flying, train, and driving times, consuming more than a few cups of coffee to keep them straight.

The Ukrainian Academy of Sciences is headquartered in Kyiv and has three subsidiaries, one of which is in Kharkiv. It doesn't have a top-secret facility on the Dnieper River. I chose that location because I needed Assonov's team to make their assault in an unpopulated area where their intrusion would go unnoticed, and he could kidnap Fedir and Olena Kuzma and get them out of the country without attracting attention. Additionally, I took liberty with the river's depth, which is only twenty-six feet, to bring the one hundred eighty feet long and twenty-one feet wide P-650 midget submarine to the fictional adjunct location of the Academy of Sciences. The P-650 requires a slightly deeper channel.

The information on how to bypass an electrified barrier is accurate. During my research, I discovered that getting past an electric fence was easier than I anticipated; the tactics ranging from shorting out the fence, which blows the circuit breaker, to intentionally setting off the alarm associated with something contacting one of the hot wires, thereby causing the security company to respond. If nothing is seen after several consecutive incidents, the security company usually chalks the triggering of the alarm to a maintenance issue. When this happens, whoever wants to enter the secure area shorts the system and hops over the fence. You can find additional information on this at (https://www.electromesh.co.za/how-criminals-bypass-electric-fences/) and (https://www.facebook.com/FidelitySecure/posts/how-criminals-bypass-electric-fencesas-homeowners-and-business-owners-it-is-our-/1072292936191971/).

My apologies to Aeroflot for my comments on their creature comforts and aircraft age. These were done for the sake of the storyline. That airline no longer flies the aging Ilyushin Il-62 aircraft, the first model of which flew in 1963. That aircraft is currently used by Belarus' Rada Airlines, North Korea's Air Koryo, and Cuba's *Cubana* de Aviación. Aeroflot has one of the youngest fleets in the world; their one hundred eighty-two aircraft—most of which are Airbus A320, Boeing 737-800, and Boeing 777-300ER, have an average age of fewer than seven years.

There are no restaurants or hotels in Oymyakon. An Overnight visitor must make prior arrangements with a resident if they intend to spend the night. As stated, Tamara Egorovna came up with the idea of renting her place, Airbnb-style, to those who wanted to brag about spending the night in the coldest inhabited settlement on earth. Her concept of Oymyakon as an adventure-tourist-destination has brought thousands of tourists to the settlement. Interestingly, each residence has central heating provided by a power station that burns wood and coal. You can read more on this by going to

(https://eugene.kaspersky.com/2021/03/10/the-one-and-only-oymyakon-the-situation-on-the-frozen-ground/) and (https://economictimes.indiatimes.com/news/international/world-news/at-50c-life-is-normal-at-the-coldest-inhabited-village-on-earth/exceptions/slideshow/62019863.cms).

While researching the coldest permanently inhabited place on earth, I learned that locals are unable to grow crops because the ground is permanently frozen, and that sixty-five percent of Russia sits on permafrost. In Siberia, the frozen ground can extend to a depth of five thousand feet. Also, forget about the criteria it takes to shut down a classroom in the United States because of cold weather. Oymyakon's school only closes if the temperature is below minus sixty-two degrees Fahrenheit. The record low for the settlement is a little over minus ninety-six degrees Fahrenheit. You can find additional information on this at (https://www.bbc.com/news/world-11875131).

The diet of the typical Oymyakon resident is reindeer, horse meat, fish, and milk from farm animals, which contains the necessary micronutrients missing from their predominantly meat diet. Also, since growing anything outdoors is impossible because of the permafrost and near-constant extreme weather, produce must be trucked in, making it a luxury item. Over time, the harshness of the environment takes its toll on residents, with the average person in Oymyakon living only to the age of sixty-nine. You can find more information on this settlement at

(https://www.atlasobscura.com/places/oymyakon-arctic-circle#:~:text=Oymyakon%20has%20no%20hotels%20or,arrange%20homestays%20with%20local%20residents.), and (https://dalgeotour.com/en/regions/magadanskaya-oblast/avtoprobeg-po-kolymskoy-trasse-magadan-ust-nera-oymyakon-yakutsk-2432-km/).

I took the information on what to wear in extremely cold environments from the following article:

(https://www.swoop-antarctica.com/travel/what-to-wear?gclid=Cj0KCQjwnP-ZBhDiARIsAH3FSReROmleCU3o-3i00gqcuQuHfvscVwwYhEsI6NC2gN_1yOQogbZt1HEaAngzEALw_wcB).

Additionally, the information on how long it takes for skin to freeze and to get frostbite at minus fifty degrees Fahrenheit was taken from a windchill chart for Canada that appeared in *Almanac* You can find this at (https://www.almanac.com/content/windchill-chart-canada).

The details on starting a vehicle in severely cold weather and the data on how different types of oil, gas, and other fluids affect their operation is accurate and was obtained from several sources. In researching how those living in the northern areas of Russia, Norway, Alaska, and so forth adapt their transports to these harsh environments, I discovered that most use engine block heaters to ensure their engine starts on demand, use synthetic oil, and put their vehicle in a shelter, if available. Ingenuity also played a large part in getting their vehicles to start. For instance, one story I read had a person draining his engine oil and keeping it warm in a large pot on his stove. He'd pour the warm oil back into the engine in the morning. It worked. A good post on how cold affects starting a vehicle is at (https://www.quora.com/Why-do-cars-fail-to-start-in-cold-temperatures). An article by Zach Reed provides a good account of how temperature affects oil. You can find this article by going to (https://vehicleanswers.com/does-motor-oil-freeze/). Information on fuel viscosity is from a February 4, 2019 article in *FleetOwner*, which you can find at (https://www.fleetowner.com/emissions–efficiency/article/21703452/diesel-gelling-and-how-to-stop-it-this-winter).

When researching what happens when someone runs in cold weather, I found an interesting article in the January 25, 2022 edition of *Runner's World* and used this to describe the effect of cold on a body. In this article, Joan Scrivanich, C.S.C.S., an exercise physiologist and a USAT and USATF certified running and triathlon coach, explains that we "have a thermoregulatory mechanism that regulates our core body temperature by increasing or decreasing heat loss and heat production within it, so we don't overheat or get too cold." Additionally, Rebekah Mayer, the National Run Program Manager at Life Time, says that "the colder it is outside, the harder your body has to work to keep your vital organs warm—and so oxygen and blood tend to be shunted away from the extremities, which can make the muscles' ability to use the oxygen less efficient than in more moderate temperatures. You can find this article by going to (https://www.runnersworld.com/uk/training/a774229/can-the-cold-slow-you-down/).

Ust Nera is a small town of five thousand on the Kolyma Highway, next to the Nera River. Most residents are engaged in gold mining, the leading industry in a region referred to as Yakutia or the Sakha Republic. The town doesn't have a train station, which I inserted for the storyline. It does have an airport consisting of one building with a half-ruined plane outside— not the best monument for nervous flyers. You can obtain more information on Ust Nera, including information from the March 12, 2020 article by Koryo Tours that I used in my manuscript, by going to (https://koryogroup.com/travel-guide/ust-nera-russia-travel-guide).

Yakutia Airlines has a fleet of thirteen airlines with an average age of seventeen years. It flies to forty destinations, including North America, Europe, and Asia. Its pilots are top-notch, flying in some of the harshest conditions in the world. My representation of them canceling a scheduled commercial flight so that they can charter the aircraft is fictional. I did this to give Wayan's team and Olena Kuzma a way to return to Moscow. Information on the Yakutia Airlines fleet can be found by going to (https://www.planespotters.net/airline/Yakutia-Airlines), and (https://en.wikipedia.org/wiki/List_of_Yakutia_destinations).

Magan Airport is a small facility seven and a half miles west of Yakutsk, and one of nine Arctic staging bases capable of handling the Tupolev Tu-22M bomber. For the sake of the storyline, I reactivated the government's presence there because I needed to get FSB agents to Ust Nera faster than was possible by taking a scheduled commercial aircraft. Getting them there quickly was essential because the lead agent needed to report to General Lazarev that they believed Olena Kuzma was on the train.

In finding a plausible way for Fedir Kuzma to avoid being taken to Kubinka Airbase, and given the scrutiny he'd be under from Assonov, I believed that only a believable medical emergency would work. After exploring many options, I settled on him taking an overdose of blood pressure medicine, thinking it was plausible that he'd be taking this medication at his age. However, in my research, I learned that this type of overdose usually takes time and could kill the person ingesting it, depending on the dosage. Nevertheless, I went with it because it made the story flow smoothly. For doctors, pharmacists, and other professionals who feel my non-existent medical/pharmacological degrees should be revoked, Mea culpa. The information on beta blockers was taken from a Mayo Clinic article, which you can find by going to (https://www.mayoclinic.org/diseases-conditions/high-blood-pressure/

in-depth/beta-blockers/art-20044522#:~:text=Beta%20
blockers%2C%20also%20known%20as,force%2C%20which%20
lowers%20blood%20pressure.), and a Mount Sinai paper, which you
can find at (https://www.mountsinai.org/health-library/poison/
beta-blockers-overdose#:~:text=A%20beta%2Dblocker%20
overdose%20can,how%20quickly%20they%20receive%20
treatment.). I took the information on troponin and heart attacks
from an October 21, 2021 article in *MedicalNewsToday* which
you can read by going to (https://www.medicalnewstoday.com/
articles/blood-tests-for-heart-attack).

I took liberties when describing the approach to the Tsentralny
Omsk Airport. Since I'm unfamiliar with the AN-140 aircraft and
the approach charts to Omsk, I guessed when the pilot would start
putting in flaps and dropping the gear. Also, I loaded the dice,
making the snowstorm so prevalent that the pilot couldn't easily
divert to his alternate airport without encountering the same or
worse conditions than at Omsk. Therefore, I committed him to
set down his aircraft in the abysmal conditions he encountered.

Mea culpa to the snow removal department at the Omsk
airport for implying their equipment is ancient and frequently
breaks down. My research has shown that's not the case and that
they use modern equipment and have well-trained personnel to
keep their ramps, runways, and taxiways clear of snow in even the
worst of conditions. I needed this excuse to give Wayan a reason
for not expecting to leave Omsk within a reasonable time and
finding another means of transport.

Active camouflage technology conceals an object from visual
detection by rapidly adapting to its surroundings. The military is
developing several competing technologies which they hope will
accomplish this. One uses OLEDs, organic light-emitting diodes,
which project images onto irregularly shaped surfaces. However,
this currently only works in one direction at a time, making it
critical to position the object to be camouflaged in the proper
position relative to the observer. Another developing technology

is phased-array optics, PAO, which uses computational holography to produce a three-dimensional hologram of background scenery on the object to be concealed. The holographic image is the scenery behind the object, irrespective of viewer distance or angle. However, all current active camouflage technologies have one flaw: they're weakened by motion Below are links to some of the materials I consulted when researching this subject. You can find these at

(https://en.wikipedia.org/wiki/Active_camouflage), (https://www.army-technology.com/analysis/military-camouflage-technology-us-russia), and (https://www.kurzweilai.net/invisibility-cloak-for-tanks-tested).

There is a skiplane version of the Cessna 207, and its specifications are as described in the novel. You can find more information on this aircraft by going to (https://aviatorinsider.com/airplane-brands/cessna-207/).

The Myachkovo Airport in Moscow is the largest of nineteen private airports for small planes, helicopters, and private flights. It and the Omsk airport do not have a skiplane landing strip or hangar, nor to the best of my knowledge, do they have skiplanes landing there. I inserted both airports into the story to give Wayan and those with him a plausible way to fly to Moscow in conditions that would ground commercial aircraft, but be faster than if they took a train. I also needed a method of getting them to Moscow in a way that would make it difficult for the FSB and military to intercept them.

Although the Aero Hotel in Omsk is real and a one-minute walk from the airport, the VIP lounge at that airport is a figment of the author's imagination.

The dacha is a cultural institution in Russia. It's estimated that sixty million Russians own dachas and go there to escape the city on weekends, holidays, and during the summer, with many located near a lake or river. However, they generally remain unused during the harsh Russian winters. You can find more on dachas, including the information contained in this novel, at (https://matadornetwork.com/read/story-behind-russian-dachas/).

The information on Russian organized crime and the Solntsevskaya Bratva was taken from the article *Russian Organized Crime,* which you can find by going to (https://irp.fas.org/world/para/docs/rusorg3.htm), and from a paper of the same title published in connection with the Stanford Model United Nations Conference 2014. You can find this at (https://web.stanford.edu/group/sias/cgi-bin/smunc/wp-content/uploads/2014/10/Russia-BG-Final.pdf). Sergei Burkov is a fictional character. The statement that the Bratva operates strictly within the confines of the Russian Federation is likewise fictitious and done for the sake of the storyline. However, this syndicate is one of the wealthiest organized crime groups in the world, with annual revenues of eight and a half billion dollars (https://fortune.com/2014/09/14/biggest-organized-crime-groups-in-the-world/), the majority of which come from drugs and human trafficking. The crime organization's heroin originates in Afghanistan and is consumed domestically, with Russian addicts buying twelve percent of the world's heroin, even though the Russian Federation accounts for only one-half percent of the world's population.

The FSBs Service of Special Communications and Information function is legally empowered to monitor all domestic telephone, internet traffic, and media—a system known as SORM, Russia's nationwide automated interception and surveillance infrastructure. This starkly contrasts with domestic law enforcement agencies in the United States and Western Europe, which must have court authorization to monitor someone. You can find more information on this system and Russia's intercept practices at (https://privacyinternational.org/blog/1296/lawful-interception-russian-approach). To my knowledge, the Indonesian government doesn't use an outdated NSA encryption system. I did this for the sake of the storyline to give a plausible way for why the FSB took so long to decrypt the conversations between Tjay and Wayan.

The information presented on extradition from Finland is correct. The Finnish government states that: *Finland may extradite a suspect or a sentenced person to a foreign state in accordance with its law even in the absence of an international obligation to that end. However, in that case extradition is discretionary. As a consequence of extradition, a suspect or sentenced person shall be transferred to the State requesting extradition. The decision to extradite binds the authorities of the requesting state. An extradited person may be prosecuted, punished or deprived of his liberty only for the offences which caused extradition. The impediments to extradition involve, among other things, extradition of nationals, political offences, time limit for prosecution and the personal circumstances of the person. Finland will not extradite own nationals other than under certain conditions to the Member States of the EU and other Nordic States.* The above information came from a publication by Finland's Ministry of Justice, which you can find at (https://oikeusministerio.fi/en/extradition).

The island of Öja is in the Gulf of Bothnia, has an area of thirty-five square miles, and a population of eight hundred. Its inhabitants have never, to my knowledge, been associated with smuggling or other illegal activity. Those implications were done for the story's sake because I needed Belevich to have someone there who'd smuggled with him in the past. That person would know how to create a makeshift landing strip on the ice at night and get him to the mainland. In contrast to smuggling, the primary source of revenue for the hard-working people on this island comes from fishing. I chose the island of Öja after extensive research because it was within the range limits of the Cessna 207 and AN-24, and was remote enough so that I could destroy the plane offshore and try and make Nazarov believe that part of it had fallen through the ice along with the bodies. It also checked the box that it was close to the Kokkola-Pietarsaari Airport, which allowed the fugitives to escape, and for the AN-24 to land when its fuel was exhausted.

Although the Lappeenranta and Kokkola-Pietarsaari airports exist and are at the distances noted within the novel, I took liberties in describing the layout of those airports, their terminals, and the existence of holding cells. I also added a skiplane runway at the Lappeenranta Airport so Belevich could land. Similarly, I required that the airport have holding cells so that the five fugitives could be arrested and held, giving the Indonesian embassy in Helsinki time to get the Kuzmas their passports and for Belevich to make a deal with Tjay and his Finnish counterpart and plan their escape.

As indicated, Finland has facial ID technology, but the infrastructure is not in place to effectively use the system. Part of the reason for the slowness of its implementation, even though the Finnish Border Guard has had the right to use this technology since 2005, is that citizens are weary that it would open the gates for "Big Brother" to constantly watch them and result in a loss of privacy. You can read more about Finland's facial recognition system at

(https://yle.fi/a/3-10818526#:~:text=The%20use%20of%20facial%20ID,individuals%20stored%20in%20official%20databases.).

Finland is the only country where all ports freeze in the winter. Because a vast majority of its imports and exports rely on its ports, icebreakers are used in the winter to create lanes to open water. Although large container ships and freighters take advantage of these, I was surprised to learn that the ferry between Finland and Estonia also uses these channels to transport passengers, vehicles, and cargo across the Gulf of Finland, a distance of fifty miles. You can find more information on these sea lanes and the ferry at (https://www.eurisy.eu/stories/

finland-allyearround-open-ports-due-to-efficient-icebreaking-services_181/) and (https://www.anadventurousworld.com/helsinki-tallinn-ferry/).

Cyberattacks into vehicle control systems increased two hundred twenty-five percent between 2018 and 2021 (https://www.israel21c.org/cyberattacks-on-cars-increased-225-in-last-three-years/), with eighty-five percent of the attacks carried out remotely. In researching these types of cyberattacks, I read a March 9, 2017 article in AutoBlog by Greg Rasa, and a subsequent article in the Washington Post that claimed the CIA could remotely hack into a vehicle and assume control. You can find this article at (https://www.autoblog.com/2017/03/09/cia-hack-car-wikileaks-assassination-surveillance-eavesdropping/). A good article on the Telecommunications Unit (TCU) and Controller Area Network bus (CAN bus) is in the June 17, 2022 publication of *VEHQ.com*. You can find this at (https://vehq.com/can-a-car-be-stopped-remotely/).

The statistics on the FSB processing of electronic and paper fingerprints apply to the FBI, not the FSB since that agency doesn't publish usage or capability numbers. You can find more about fingerprint processing in testimony made on March 30, 2004 by Michael Kirkpatrick, the FBIs Assistant Director in Charge, Criminal Justice Information Services, when he spoke before the House Judiciary Committee. You can see this by going to (https://archives.fbi.gov/archives/news/testimony/fbi-fingerprint-program).

The information on a vehicle's suspension came from a September 26, 2022 article in *OSVehicle* by Abdul, which discusses the suspension of sports cars. You can read this article by going to (https://www.osvehicle.com/the-importance-of-stiff-suspension-in-sports-cars/). Because Wayan was driving in a semi-reckless manner while attempting to catch Nazarov's vans, I used the information from this article to put more detail into how the SUV reacted rather than simply saying it skidded or bounced. Hopefully, it enhanced the authenticity of the chase.

Go to alanrefkin.com for photos of me at many locations mentioned in the novel. *Story Settings* will show you the venues, weapons, aircraft, ships, etc., referenced in *The Defector*.

ABOUT THE AUTHOR

Alan Refkin has written thirteen previous works of fiction and is the co-author of four business books on China, for which he received Editor's Choice Awards for *The Wild Wild East* and *Piercing the Great Wall of Corporate China*. In addition to the Gunter Wayan private investigator novels, he's written the Matt Moretti-Han Li action-adventure thrillers and the Mauro Bruno detective series. He and his wife Kerry live in southwest Florida, where he's working on his next Gunter Wayan novel.

Printed in the United States
by Baker & Taylor Publisher Services